Praise for Michelle M. Pillow's
*Faery Queen*

"We could all use a little bit of Euphoria now and again. ...Michelle M. Pillow is per magic."

~ *Sensual Reads*

"Those who are hardy and brave will applaud this tale of love."

~ *RT Magazine, May 2007*

"We could all use a little bit of Euphoria. ...Michelle M. Pillow is pure magic."

~ *Sensual Reads, March 2008*

Rating: 5 Books! "Faery Queen is a rich enthralling story, filled with paranormal creatures, love and lust. I was fascinated right from page one... Add to this the magic and the battle between good and evil, and you have the ingredients for a great story."

~ *LASR, May 2009*

# Look for these titles by
*Michelle M. Pillow*

*Now Available:*

*Realm Immortal*

King of the Unblessed (Book 1)

Faery Queen (Book 2)

Stone Queen (Book 3)

Talons: Seize the Hunter

*Print Anthology*

Talons

# Faery Queen

*Realm Immortal Book Two*

*Michelle M. Pillow*

A Samhain Publishing, Ltd. publication.

Samhain Publishing, Ltd.
577 Mulberry Street, Suite 1520
Macon, GA 31201
www.samhainpublishing.com

Faery Queen – Realm Immortal Book Two

Print ISBN: 978-1-60504-514-6
Digital ISBN: 978-1-60504-508-5

Editing by Angela James
Cover by Natalie Winters



First Samhain Publishing, Ltd. electronic publication: September 2006
Second Samhain Publishing, Ltd. electronic publication: March 2009
First Samhain Publishing, Ltd. print publication January 2007
Second Samhain Publishing, Ltd. print publication: January 2010

# Dedication

To my mother, a true queen who saves lives and makes the world a better place. For your strength of heart and bravery of soul. I love you.

# Note from the Author

Though they can be read separately, author recommends reading Realm Immortal books in order of release. For details please visit her website www.michellepillow.com.

# Prologue

*Silver Palace of the Faeries, Kingdom of Feia, Immortal Realm 1407 AD*

It was ill-advised to incur the wrath of a faery, but it was most foolish to do so of a faery queen. And if that wrath came from a disappointed heart, then all would have to pay the price.

Queen Tania of the Faeries felt herself slipping into the black abyss that had become her world. Her heart was broken and each day a small piece of it fell away into darkness. Faeries were not meant for darkness. They were meant to see only pretty things, to experience good and light. Tania, by her very nature, wasn't equipped to deal with the shadows of unpleasant emotions. She didn't understand them.

Many reasons were speculated to be the cause of the change in her. The most obvious was the war that raged outside the silver walls of her palace. It was a war fought between the blessed Kingdom of Tegwen and the unblessed Kingdom of Valdis, but more poignantly it was a war fought between two brothers—unblessed King Merrick and blessed King Ean. Merrick had once been destined for the Tegwen throne, but mysterious events had brought him to rule Valdis instead. Some claimed Merrick resented his brother for taking the kingdom that should have been his and, out of spite, had stolen away one of King Ean's blessed wards from the mortal realm.

That human, Lady Juliana, was now Merrick's queen. But she was merely an excuse, not the full reason for the war.

Being a faery, Tania hated war and the destruction it brought to the land. But, as a lesser queen, she had no say in wars. If the higher King Ean called her to join in battle she would be compelled to do so. Luckily, the elves never called the faeries for such things. Faeries were useless in battle.

Light faeries, *her* faeries, believed in love and happy endings. They could only exist on good and pleasant thoughts, and their existence helped to balance the natural magic of both realms. The faeries woke the land after a harsh winter and tucked it in with the fall. Their magic gave the delicate flower strength to grow in the hard, impossible ground.

It wasn't the war that wrung all pleasure from her heart, but the event was tied to what had. When Merrick took Juliana, the noblewoman's brothers had come to the immortal realm to rescue her. There was one brother in particular, Hugh, Earl of Bellemare. He was valiant for a human, brave and strong, bold and decisive, if not a wee bit irritatingly set in his ways.

The story of Merrick kidnapping Juliana against all odds, against the workings of his very nature as the Unblessed King, had captured the attention of her faery court. Tania had wanted to be a part of that story, to be known as the queen who helped bring the lovers together. And she did, purposefully shoving Juliana through a portal to Merrick's bedchambers. Juliana had come to Feia with Hugh, their brother Sir Thomas and Sir Nicholas, the son of Juliana's dead fiancé. Tania had only meant to detain Lord Bellemare and his traveling companions so that King Merrick would have time to pursue his lover without their interference. However, in doing so, the faery queen had fallen in love with the mortal earl, and Lord Bellemare had fallen in love with her, or so she had thought.

His words were as clear as the day he said them. *'First, I rescue my sister. Then, I'll be back to settle with you.'*

She waited, as he rode off to do battle on the side of the blessed army to win back his sister. The battle ended, Hugh survived, Juliana chose to be the Unblessed Queen and was safe for the time being, but the earl never came back to keep his promise to her. Nay, he went back to his home in the mortal realm, his beloved Bellemare.

Tania sat in the center of a round chamber with her legs crossed, waiting as she had done for over a year. Like the rest of her palace, the walls were carved with intricate silver designs, decorated with the ancient symbols of her people, concentrating all the powers of the faeries. Positioned on a stone island in the middle of a round divination pool, near the water's edge, she contemplated Hugh's fate.

Unfisting her hand she looked down at the two strands of hair, which she carried always on her person. They were dark, sinfully so against her paler skin. Thin lines had grown along her hand from where she often held the hairs, becoming permanent marks on her flesh. The lines wound along her arm and shoulder, curling like tiny dark brown vines up her neck and spreading over her chest until one side of her body was marred by the darkness. Even her wings, which had once been the most beautiful of transparent white with silver threading, had started to turn dark, the threading black.

Tania leaned forward to the pool to see the reflection of what her face had become. The tallest of the faeries, she still had her slender figure, though dark brown strands had begun to sprout down one side of her blonde hair. She kept the locks parted in the middle, held down by a silver and diamond crown. It created an odd contrast between the light and dark, revealing to all the torment inside her soul.

Some of her court whispered the change came about because she'd gone mad. Others said it was because of the war between the blessed and unblessed, because of the flowers trampled under soldier's feet and the trees burned and scarred by the breath of warrior dragons. The war was a good presumption and did depress her spirits some, but it was not her true reason.

Then others still claimed it was because she was dying, like the faery magic she carried. None of them suspected the truth, none knew that it was merely an outside reflection of the hate and anger she harbored deep inside.

Well, that wasn't necessarily true. Queen Tania had a feeling one person suspected her plight. King Lucien of the Damned. The weakness within her would be clear to a demon like him. He was one of the three high kings of the immortal realm, ruling on equal ground with King Ean and King Merrick.

Aye, Lucien knew what was happening to her. As she watched the earl, she'd seen signs that Lucien's demons were crossing between the realms near Bellemare. The Damned King was biding his time until she weakened enough to let her guard slip and Tania didn't know if she'd bother to stop him when the occasion came for her to act.

Her hand trembling, she took a single hair and lifted it. Why hadn't she stolen more from Hugh when he'd been in her home? There were only two strands left and that meant she could only see the earl two more times without going to him directly. Tania had thought of making the trip across worlds, but in truth the mortal realm frightened her. Her magic was lessened there and she'd never walked as a human or without her full powers.

A hairy fish with sharp teeth swam near the water's surface, disrupting her reflection. Tania dropped the hair in the small ripple the fish created. "What better thing does he do this day instead of keeping his word to me? Why is Bellemare so special when compared to my silver palace?"

Suddenly, a large wall of light formed before her, made up of small, colorful squares. In each box was a different scene of the mortal keep of Bellemare. Her eyes went to Hugh and she felt a deep pain shoot through her chest. She'd watched him often and though his smiles were rare, they were the most handsome thing she'd ever seen. Even a year later he could still make her wings flutter. A year wasn't a long time in a faery's life, but for Tania the days had been endless and it felt like an eternity.

She looked at Hugh, remembering his smell, his feel. Tiny lights erupted from her wings, pheromones attesting to her longing for him. Her magic showered over the pool, sitting like bright dots on the water's surface before sinking into the depths. For a briefest moment, the swarms of fish became illuminated, but then the inky obscurity consumed them again.

Tania's wings flapped and she lifted off the stone island, moving to float near Hugh's oversized face. By the appearance of everything, it was night in Bellemare and the keep was at rest. Why did he sit up?

Firelight caressed one of his stubbled cheeks. He appeared tired. She couldn't tell what he was doing, but suddenly, his eyes turned and it was as if he looked directly at her.

Reaching forward, she tried to touch his cheek, but her hand merely fell through the image of him. It was torture to be this close to him without being able to feel his skin against hers. Like his three siblings, he had dark brown hair that gleamed in the sunlight, high cheekbones and proud features. She ran her finger down the slope of his nose. Hugh, and the youngest of Bellemare's noble family, William, had brown eyes that could look as dark as the stone of the Black Palace. The others, Juliana and Thomas, had blue eyes the color of the night sky.

Lids lowered over her eyes as she leaned forward, her lips pursed to touch his. His dark gaze pierced through her, causing another ache, as her lips only met air. Twice he'd kissed her and she longed for the third. Her skin itched and she knew the black lines grew, stretching and vining their way up her neck to decorate her cheek. They encircled her navel and grew over a breast before stopping.

Movement in another square caught her eye. She frowned, drifting to the side to study a dim panel. A brownie slept, his mouth wide open as he snored. The two small holes of his nostrils expanded and contracted, vibrating with each breath. Straw stuck to the creature's tattered green and blue suit and she thought to detect more of it on his dirty face. He was Bellemare's household brownie, unseen by most of the humans in the mortal realm. Being magical, Tania had no problem seeing all creatures in the castle.

A shadow crossed over the brownie, giving Tania the barest peek of a leg. An overwhelming sense that the shadow did not belong in Bellemare struck her full force. It was hard to tell what manner of creature the intruder was, though it was much bigger than a brownie or spright. Her stomach tensed and she glanced over the small boxes, trying to see if she could catch another glimpse of the figure.

She passed several panels filled with Bellemare's empty halls, a garden gnome working in the courtyard, guards awake and posted along the castle battlements, a view of the entire castle from far away. The castle itself was beautiful and the family within it had been greatly blessed with fertile lands, good health, incredible luck and fine looks. The home sat atop a mound of earth and rock, towering a good fifty feet above the bailey, over a courtyard. The only way in and out of the yard was through the front gatehouse.

Tania searched more panels, looking over the inner courtyard for signs of an intrusion. A couple of mortals made love behind the stables, a man was passed out on the doorstep of the small brewery, workshops were empty except for the occasional magical creature hard at work during the night hours, helping the mortals that didn't know they existed. Stopping near the panel of the chapel, Tania frowned. Now that was something which should not have been there.

# Chapter One

*Bellemare Castle, England, Mortal Realm*

"Accursed faery," Lord Bellemare mumbled as he tried to push Queen Tania out of his mind. But as a year had proven, forgetting her wasn't so easily done. It wasn't unusual for the faery queen to enter his thoughts, plaguing him with questions of "what if" and filling him with renewed anger at what she'd done to him—or more to the point what she had not done. Yet there were times, like tonight, when the memory of her felt so real it was as if he could see her floating before him, sense her nearness, so close he could almost feel her in his arms. He imagined her hair rippling like linens in the wind, her body nearly as translucent as the breeze. Her delicate face blurred and shadowed, and her round blue eyes were deceitfully innocent. The color reminded him of a stormy sea, a description that fit her temperament as well—ever changing like the waves.

Running his hand through his hair, Hugh grabbed fistfuls only to pull hard as he growled in frustration. "Get out of my thoughts, wretched creature! I want to forget you. Leave me in peace."

*Leave me in peace.*

Hugh needed his mind to focus on the matter at hand. His childhood home was slowly falling apart. He felt it in his bones. The signs were small, could be marked as merely bad luck or coincidence, but they were there. Ever since he came back from his journey into the Otherworld, he'd known his home was changing for the worse. One of his greatest fears was that he would not be able to stop whatever was happening.

At first, he contributed the feelings of impending despair to Juliana's absence. His sister was a bright spot in all their lives and when she left, so did the radiance of her presence. He lied to his people—another example of how things had changed—telling them she'd married a far off lord. It wasn't a complete lie, but he wouldn't make excuses for misleading them to think southern France when he knew she really resided in another realm.

Then there were the horses. The Bellemare family was renowned for their breeding abilities, producing some of the finest horses in the entire world. It was a reputation they had taken pride in for generations. There were many elements to the breeds, passed from father to son over the years. The animals were an ancient mix of bloodlines, a crossbreeding of French trotters and hunters for stamina, with the intelligence of a Holstein Warmblood and the jumping abilities of a Lipizzaner. Not once could Hugh remember a horse being stillborn, not until that evening. Two prized mares had given birth to dead foals. With three unformed legs on one and an uncovered skull on the other, it was best the poor animals didn't live. Regardless, the event hung over the keep like a bad omen. Three other mares were pregnant, about ready to drop, and everyone in the castle was anxious.

"So ashamed I am, my lord," came a small whisper. "So ashamed."

Hugh frowned, sitting up in his chair. He'd been staring into his fireplace, about to drift off into the world of dreams when he heard the words. The earl glanced over the dark green coverlet on his bed. It was embroidered with a horse to match the Bellemare crest—a black stallion statant on a field of green. The mattress was empty, yet he swore that was where the voice had come from.

"King Alwyn, rest him, ordered us here to your keep to watch after you and I have failed with the horses."

"Rees?" Hugh sighed heavily and his drowsy head cleared. He recognized the spright's voice. "Show yourself. You know I do not like when you lurk about unseen."

As if stepping out of some undetectable fog, the Bellemare spright appeared. Rees was only as tall as Hugh's knee with short, unkempt brown hair and blue eyes almost too big for his small face. It still made Hugh uneasy to see the magical creatures appear and disappear. Though he decreed they make themselves known to him if in his presence, how could he ever be sure he wasn't being spied on in private moments? Until Juliana had been kidnapped by King Merrick, he hadn't known such things existed.

"What happened to your new tunic?" Hugh asked, seeing the small man didn't have a shirt on. The spright had been in a tattered, bright green tunic until Hugh presented him with the one he now should have been wearing—a darker green with the Bellemare crest over the heart. Rees thought the clothing a great honor, one he bragged about to the other creatures. Hugh didn't tell the spright, but he'd only given him the clothes to make Rees more presentable.

Being earl he was used to respect, but the spright's attention went beyond that into blind adoration. Rees had attached himself to the earl, following him around the keep, popping onto his shoulders during the day, trying to sleep at the foot of his bed near the fireplace. Often, he'd appear, waving and blinking his big eyes behind whomever Hugh was talking to. It was an awful distraction, startling to say the least.

"So sorry I am. I do not deserve to be your spright. Two charges..." The spright's big eyes teared up and he shook his head, burying it in his hands. "I was given charge of the horses and for hundreds of years I did my job well, but now..." He sighed heavily. "Now, I must be past my use."

"Such things happen," Hugh lied, uncomfortable, never sure how to receive the attachment. In truth, things like this never happened at Bellemare.

"Not on my watch. Not when you're blessed."

"Would there be a reason for King Ean to take off his grandfather's blessing on Bellemare? On us? Is he displeased with us?" Hugh paused. King Ean of Tegwen's grandfather had blessed Hugh's ancestor after the man had saved the king's daughter and married her. The elf princess had become mortal and eventually died as mortals do, but the blessing stood. Was Ean displeased with the fact that Juliana had married his unblessed brother? "Have we given him cause for anger?"

"He has said nothing to me." Rees sniffed loudly. "He has been busy with the war from what I've heard."

Hugh had thought of that as well. Was the war distracting King Ean, taking away power from the blessing? The earl didn't know enough about the immortal realm to discern how exactly a blessing might work.

"Nay, my lord," Rees continued. "I fear this is my fault. I understand if you do not want me anymore."

Hugh cleared his throat, uncomfortable. "Ah, I..."

Rees sniffed again, a loud, womanly sound.

"I still, ah, require your services," Hugh said, trying to be diplomatic. It went against his nature to say, "I still want you", to a spright.

"Even after this?" Rees insisted, giving the first sign of a smile.

"I do not think it is you. Something is not right at Bellemare, Rees." It was the first time Hugh had voiced his fears out loud and he wondered why he would be compelled to do so in front of the spright and not his own brothers, Thomas and William. "I can feel it in my bones."

Just then, a loud crash sounded in the hall followed by the hammering of footsteps as someone ran toward his door. Hugh stood, waving his hand at Rees. The spright instantly disappeared. Running to his trunk, he grabbed his sword off the top before hurrying to open the door.

"Ho!" Hugh yelled, armed and ready. He leveled the tip of his sword down the hall. He had yet to change his clothes for the night and still wore his long, green overtunic and breeches. A loud, piercing scream echoed over him. He flinched, instantly removing the tip of his blade from the direction of the hysterical serving maid. "What goes on here?"

"Oh, my lord," the woman answered. "You must come down to the bailey. The devil comes to Bellemare."

*Who now?*

Hugh was less alarmed than the woman by her declaration. His first thought was of his brother-by-marriage, King Merrick of the Unblessed. The man did have the manners of a devil about him.

The woman's wide violet gaze met his. He was sure he would remember seeing a woman with eyes like that in his castle, but he had little time to try and place who she might be as she trembled before him, stumbling forward. Hugh automatically lifted his arm in a protective gesture, catching her against his body. The maid pressed against this chest, burying her head. The shock of her soft figure against his harder one made him tense as a sudden wave of desire washed through him. She smelled clean, sweet and made soft noises in the back of her throat—the kind of breathy, fragile sounds distinctive of the female sex.

He'd been celibate since meeting Tania, not trusting any woman enough to let her get close. But now the sudden press of feminine curves clouded his mind, stirring the all-too-neglected part of his male awareness. He became conscious of her breasts, the nearness of her thighs. For a moment, he considered kissing her, pushing her against the passageway wall and lifting her skirts. It wouldn't take much to meet his release and the woman was beautiful. Hugh took a deep breath and instead patted her awkwardly on the shoulder, keeping his sword hand to the side. Now was not the occasion for such carnal pastimes.

"I saw him, my lord," the woman continued.

"Saw who?" His voice was strained.

"The devil!" she cried in terror, moving torturously against him.

"Who is the devil?" Hugh tried his best to walk down the hall in the direction she'd come from. The woman clung to him, making it hard to move without brushing up against her.

"Hugh?" A shirtless Thomas appeared at the end of the hall, his overlong dark hair flopping around his head. He too carried a sword. His eyes narrowed in surprise to see Hugh holding the woman. Thomas stopped and pointed back the way he'd come. "Do you...? Should I...?"

"She has seen the devil." Hugh forcefully put the woman away from him. Thomas' face fell in disappointment. It was no secret his two brothers had tried to tempt him by bringing pretty women to the keep. Was this woman one such temptation? Did they seek to bring forth the protective instincts inside him with the frail, pretty maid? He thought of Queen

Tania and the violet-eyed woman's beauty paled in comparison.

*The faery witch has ruined me!*

"The devil?" William joined them at a slower pace. He looked like Hugh had as a younger man, with the same hair and dark eyes, though William wore his locks longer, letting them hang shaggily around his head. He also wore brown robes, a custom he'd picked up while studying at a monastery. Well, the family had thought he was at a monastery, when in truth he'd been apprenticing to be a wizard. Stopping, his eyes went to the woman curiously. "The real devil? Nay, that is not possible. The real devil cannot cross over—"

"William." Hugh glared at the youngest brother in warning. The servants didn't know about the immortal realm, beyond their everyday superstitions, and he had every intention of keeping it that way. The last thing he wanted was all of Bellemare running away out of fear. Or worse, accusing his family of witchery and devil worship.

All it would take was one of Bellemare's enemies to spread a rumor that he'd sold his soul for good horse stock and riches, before the church would intervene, excommunicate him and steal his lands. Bellemare was the envy of many and whereas he demanded respect with his position, Hugh also walked a very fine line with other nobles. All many of them would need was one excuse to try and take what was his.

"I know what I saw." Tears poured over the woman's cheeks. "The devil waits outside the gate. He has come to Bellemare. Why else do you think the horses died?"

"What?" William's expression fell. "What horses? What is she talking about?"

"We lost two foals a couple hours ago," Hugh answered. "Stillborn."

"But that never happens," Thomas said. "Not in my entire

life."

"Nor mine," said Hugh. "Nor in the life of our father."

"Where is this devil, woman?" William moved toward her. She managed to compose herself, though she still shook. "Where did you see him?"

"The front gate, waiting to be let in," she said.

"Did you let him in?" Thomas asked in alarm.

"Nay!" she spat, as if he were crazy for thinking such a thing.

"Did he speak? Did he say what he wanted?" William grabbed her arm.

The woman yelped and pulled out of his grasp. She signed her chest with the cross and looked at Hugh. "I do not converse with devils, my lord."

"William, stay with," Hugh struggled, but still couldn't place who the woman might be, "*her*. Thomas, come with me to the gate."

Hugh began to lead the way, when the woman said, "I do not need him to watch me. I'll go to the chapel."

"William, escort her to the chapel," Hugh ordered, not stopping to argue with her over the matter. The last thing he wanted was a maid running around his keep screaming about devils. When they were away from her, heading down a stairwell lit by torches toward the great hall of Bellemare, he said, "It is odd, but I do not feel as panicked as I would have a year ago hearing her say that."

"I know," Thomas agreed. "My first thought was King Merrick."

"Mine, too." Hugh paused to grab an unlit torch off the wall as they entered the hall. He crossed to the fireplace and thrust it in the low flames. An orange glow came from the end of the torch, giving them better light to see by. He shared a concerned look with his brother. Mayhap it really was Merrick.

"Juliana," they said in unison, drawing the same conclusion. If Merrick had come to the castle their sister might be in some sort of trouble. Had the war reached their sister? Had something happened to her? It had been so long since they'd heard anything from her—almost a year in fact and that was a letter telling them of the child she carried. There had been no news since.

Hugh was spurred into action, quickly weaving around the permanent dining tables to the other side of the hall. Thomas was right behind him. Going to a second stairwell that led outside to the inner courtyard, the brothers raced down and ran toward a tall stone and timber wall that guarded the main part of the keep. Hurrying through the opening in the wall, they went to the front gate. A second wall wound around the outside of the castle grounds. It was shorter than the inside wall, but still high enough to provide protection. A couple of the guards stood on the battlements like stone fixtures, their bodies unmoving and outlined by moonlight. At the sight of the two nobles, they sprung into action, hurrying along the top edge to meet them near the gate.

"Simon," Hugh hollered, looking up at one of the men. "Have there been visitors?"

"Nay, my lord." Simon, the guard, glanced across the top of the gate to the other man.

"Nay, my lord," Tobias, the other guard answered.

"Check along the wall," Hugh ordered. "Look for a man outside the castle."

The guards obeyed.

"Hugh, wait," said Thomas. "We have it wrong. It cannot be Merrick. If it were Merrick, why would he wait outside the gate?

Why wouldn't he just come in? He is family."

"Family by marriage," Hugh corrected. It pained him to admit it, but Thomas was right. Merrick didn't seek permission from them to do things. He would have just appeared, not wait for an invitation.

"What of the other? The King of the Damned?" Thomas asked.

"King Lucien cannot come to our world," Hugh said, thinking of the Damned King. "William said he is trapped on his side. But it could be one of his minions I suppose."

"Mayhap it's nothing," Thomas answered. "Methinks the woman wanted some attention. Either that or the servants snuck into the brewery again, heard of the horses and scared themselves with things that aren't there. You know as well as I how the night can play tricks on a person's vision. Once, at tournament, methought I saw a two foot man playing a fiddle. It turned out to be a fallen log."

"With our family, and what we have discovered follows us around this keep unseen, it could well have been a two foot creature playing a fiddle that you later mistook for a log."

"Ah, good point." Thomas nodded.

"You know as well as I that there are things we cannot know." Hugh looked around the outer courtyard for a sign of what the woman had been talking about.

"And you know as well as I that if this same woman had come to us two years ago and said the same thing, we would not be out here chasing imaginary devils." Thomas pointed the tip of the sword toward the top of the castle. "You would be up there, comforting the pretty wench as you tried to get her to play with your..." Thomas paused and swung his sword so it pointed at Hugh's hips. "Little devil."

"Things have changed. Demons do exist, as does magic. We

know that now and must act accordingly." Hugh shot his brother a bemused look. "And *little* is hardly the word for my devil."

Thomas gave a short chuckle. "You keep neglecting it and it will most likely jump out of your breeches and leave you for good."

"Thomas," Hugh warned, shaking his head as he tried not to laugh at the imagery. How could he tell his brother that when he closed his eyes, all he thought about was the faery queen? Even now, after the time that had passed, he wanted to both strangle her and kiss her, but such women were not for his doing either to. She was a queen, a faery, a magical being that flew around her castle taunting him. He was better off without her. Now, if only he could convince his body of the same thing. "Do not pretend the knowledge of the immortal realm hasn't affected you. You're the one who has been having nightmares since we arrived back."

Hugh gave him a teasing smile. Thomas rolled his eyes, and grumbled, "Bad dreams are one thing and they do not rule my life. At least I usually have a warm body in my bed to soothe me when I awake from them."

Hugh grimaced. "I have no wish to hear your lecture. I have graver things on my mind than bedding the fairer sex."

"It's not your fault Juliana chose to stay," Thomas said. The two were close, having grown up together, trained together, fought together. Hugh wasn't surprised that his brother read him so well.

*Nay,* Hugh thought, *it is Tania's. She sent our sister to the Unblessed King's palace. She delivered her into Merrick's hands and detained us from going to rescue her before it was too late, before she became so warped, so tangled in Merrick's dark web.*

"She does not belong there." Hugh took a deep breath. This

was a worn conversation that went nowhere. "She's not one of them. Her heart is too good."

"According to William, Merrick's not all bad. Mayhap our sister sees that. She chose him, Hugh." Thomas lifted his hand, motioning helplessly to the side. "She loves Merrick."

"But he does not love her. You heard him when we were there, as well as I. She asked him if he loved her and he said nay. I know she was upset about her fiancé's death. We all know Lord Eadward's undoing wasn't her fault, but—"

"Nay," Thomas interrupted. "I daresay she was more upset by Nicholas killing his father than her fiancé dying. She did not love Lord Eadward, merely knew him as a friend of our father."

Sir Nicholas, their childhood friend, had been possessed by a demon and driven to kill his father, Lord Eadward. Nicholas was susceptible to the demon because he was in love with Juliana and jealous that his father should have her. Their sister never realized his feelings until it was too late. Hugh was convinced if Juliana knew Nicholas loved her, she would have chosen him, gotten married and none of them would have ever known the Otherworld truly existed. Now Nicholas was dead, killed by the demon that had possessed him.

"Then we are agreed," Hugh concluded. Thomas frowned, confused. "Juliana stayed as a self-punishment. She blames herself for Lord Eadward's death. I should never have arranged the marriage."

"It's not your fault. We all wanted her to live close to Bellemare and with Lord Eadward bordering our lands she would have been nearby. We all agreed on it." Thomas patted his shoulder. "William and I carry just as much blame for the decision."

"Nay, I asked your consent but in the end the decision was mine to make. This title is my responsibility to bear and, as head of the family, the blame for any decision made is mine." Hugh's gaze continued to search the gate, as he listened for signs of movement. He detected nothing.

"I wish Nicholas would have come forward with his feelings. This all could have been avoided." Thomas also watched the gate.

"I should have guessed it—the way he would lecture her when we were young, the way he followed her around the castle. I should have known." Hugh gripped his sword in frustration. "Methinks she blames me as well. Why else hasn't she contacted us since right after we left her? Methinks she would at least tell us of the child she carried."

The thought of his sister bearing an unblessed child worried him. What kind of being would the baby be? Half human, half unblessed creature? And why hadn't she sent word about its birth? The silence was unbearable.

"Perchance there has been no way for her to send—" Thomas began, only to be cut off by the guard.

"My lord, there is naught but night," Simon called down from the wall.

"All's well," yelled Tobias.

Hugh raised his hand in acknowledgement. "Keep your eyes open and the gate closed. No one gets in or out. We will sort it out in the morning."

"Aye, my lord," the guards answered in unison, not questioning even though Hugh knew they had to be curious about the late night search.

"Let's go check on the mares." Hugh motioned for Thomas to come with him. "Then we can deal with our devil-seeing woman."

"I have one idea as to how you can deal with her." Thomas

laughed.

"Do not make me strangle you, brother."

"I believe what you say." William kept his voice low as he gave the pretty maid a come-hither smile. While he was away for five years apprenticing, his family had believed he was on the verge of taking religious orders. How wrong they had been. Anything but a pious young man, William knew he was the attraction of many women—much to the astonishment of his older brothers. But, his success wasn't really a mystery. His boyish charms drew the women like bees to a field of flowers and his monkish robes didn't hurt his chances either. The fairer sex liked the idea of the forbidden. "I said, I believe what you say about the devil."

The woman turned her violet eyes to him, shaded partly by the silky strands of her dark hair as they fell over her forehead. He'd never seen eyes that color on a human woman before and suspected she was something different from the beginning—if not in whole than in part.

Hugh and Thomas were new to the ways of the immortal realm, still taking people and things as they saw them to be. They saw this woman, in her servant's gown, inside a castle impenetrable by human forces and they thought "servant". They heard that there was a devil outside the gate and they assumed that such a creature would stay there until he was let in. William knew better. Being in the immortal realm had taught him that things were not as they appeared and to look beyond what was right in front of him. If this woman was not a full-blooded human and if she knew anything about demons, why send his brothers to the front gate?

"Do you now?" She pursed her lips and stepped closer.

William swallowed, instantly aroused by her nearness. He licked his lips, hearing the telltale husky quality to her seductive voice. Eagerly he nodded. "Aye."

They were in the great hall, alone, with no one in sight. He glanced around to be sure. The fire burned behind her, outlining her slender form. There were plenty of places for them to disappear to. Along one wall a table set up from the rest of the hall on a platform. It was where the family dined with honored guests. They could hide beneath it in the shadows, should she be willing. Blue tapestries hung on the wall, along with the Bellemare crest. How angry would Hugh be if he tore them down for a bed to lay her on?

On second thought, perhaps he should take her somewhere else.

"Then you know the devil?" Her long lashes fluttered over her eyes.

"You are beautiful."

"Have you seen the devil?" She stepped closer.

"I really want to bed you." William leaned his face toward hers.

"Have you slept with the devil?" Her eyes hardened, but William was too far gone in lust to react properly.

"Are you offering?" He started to close his eyes.

The woman lifted her hand and pressed it to her lips. Pulling it away, she blew him a kiss over the short distance. "I have done all those things."

William felt her kiss like a cold blast across the face, paralyzing him. A short, feminine-sounding scream echoed over the hall and he realized it came from his lips. Weakly, he collapsed on the floor, unable to move from his uncomfortable position as the woman kneeled over him. He tried with all his power, but was unable to pull away.

"William the Wizard, I have a message for your brothers. The devil is coming to Bellemare and he is after your souls. Your magical guard is too lax. If I can get this close to you, he will have no trouble getting much closer." She leaned over, kissing his lips. He felt another cold wave where she touched him before his entire world faded to black.

Heinic hefted the sack of vegetables, dragging them unhurriedly across the long courtyard and up the steep stairwell, lumbering along at a slow and steady pace on his squat legs. The mortal world wasn't built to accommodate gnomes, but he was sent by the King of the Blessed himself to work the land and, as Bellemare's garden gnome, he took his duty seriously. It was a good piece of land, too, his garden.

It was night, the air perfect for picking. The humans knew nothing about vegetables or herbs, or growing mud for that matter. They thought they could simply harvest whenever they felt like it. But that wasn't how gardens worked. Each vegetable, each herb had its perfect time to be picked.

Heinic was a little man with the rounded cheeks his race was known for. But unlike the drab woodland gnomes, his kind celebrated color in their gardens and in their clothes. His jacket was red over a bright green shirt. It was impossible to get colors like that in the mortal realm. He had a wife back home who sent them to him. A fine wife she was too, at least from what he remembered of her.

Hearing a hiccup as he dragged his bag into the pantry, he

glanced up at the barrel of ale. Giles waved down at him, liquor dripping off his long, nimble fingers to land on Heinic's head. The gnome frowned, swiping off his hat and shaking it dry.

"Ah, Giles," Heinic grumbled, glaring at the drunken household brownie. Giles' flat face glistened from where he'd dunked himself in ale and the two small holes of his nose fluttered with each heavy breath. "Be it necessary?"

"Aye." The brownie hiccupped. "I am checking the ale. Would not want any to get a drink of the sour."

"And I be fightin' a dragon," the gnome retorted derisively, pulling his bag across the floor to rest with the other vegetables.

"You are?" Giles' eyes got wide.

Heinic snorted.

"Lady Juliana used to tell us stories about dragons," Giles mused, his voice wistful. "I miss her. I wish she would come back."

"As do we all," the gnome said, waddling back to look up at the brownie. "Well, give us a drink."

"Oh, aye!" the brownie lifted a finger. "Come on up, the ale is warm tonight!"

Heinic pushed the side of his nose and pointed up. His body dissipated as he was carried by magic to the rim of the barrel. Then, sitting along the side, his sore feet dipped in warm ale, he sighed. Giles took off his small cap, filled it with ale and handed it up.

"Ah, there you be," Heinic said in pleasure as he took it, bringing the hat to his lips for a drink.

"Oh, did you hear that?" Giles' small eyes widened as his body dropped down into the barrel.

"Ach, forget it, the mortals cannot see us."

"There are more than mortals coming through the pantry,"

Giles said. “It’s been eventful tonight.”

Heinic leaned over to look toward the far door. “I do not hear—”

“Down!” Giles said, pulling his arm. Heinic fell into the ale with a big splash. The liquid seeped into his clothes, surely staining his nice bright green shirt. Sinking to the bottom of the barrel like a stone, he frowned, holding his breath as he looked up through the thin layer of ale that covered his head. The liquor was dark and he couldn’t see. Giles’ feet pumped near his face only to skim his shoulder as if trying to find a perch on the gnome. Heinic pushed his foot aside.

Giles reached down and pulled him up. Heinic sputtered and swiped his wet face with one hand while holding the side with the other. Putting his finger along his nose, he tried to get out of the barrel. The liquid made him too heavy and all he did was bob up and down.

“That was close. The lady almost saw you.” The brownie nodded enthusiastically.

“Mortal’s cannot see us, you toadstool!” Heinic grumbled. “Now get me out of here!”

“I told you, there are more than mortals wandering about the castle these nights,” Giles said, even as he moved to help the gnome out of the ale.

“I asked him to do one simple thing and he cannot even get that right,” Hugh grumbled. They’d gone to the chapel only to discover William had never arrived. He knew that most likely his youngest brother had seduced the woman into his bed, but it didn’t stop Hugh from worrying about him. “Methinks it is time I took account of the castle again. I cannot remember ever seeing that maid before tonight."

"You mean..." Thomas frowned. "You do not know her?"

"I haven't paid much mind to the women here as of late. Why? Don't you?"

"Nay, brother. I have not seen her." Thomas patted his arm. "I am sure she is related to one of the field workers, come to work at the castle. We will ask the steward in the morning."

The main hall was empty as they stepped across it, but the fire still burned. Hugh didn't want to bother with it, so he decided to let the flames go out on their own, even though the hall was already warm and had no need of heat.

"No one is getting past the guards, whether it is to come in or to leave. William can take care of himself."

"The talk of devils has got me thinking." Hugh didn't want to risk losing William like he had Juliana. A large part of him still felt as if he'd failed her, even though she claimed to be happy in her choice. "I keep remembering how easily Juliana was taken from us."

"Any mortal threat will have to come through the gate or over the wall, both of which are well-manned. As for a magical threat, well, William knows more protection spells than either of us could dream up in a dozen lifetimes." Thomas went to the stairwell, suppressing a yawn.

"Aye, you are right," Hugh nodded. It was late and most of the castle had been asleep for hours. "Let us get some rest. You can help me wring William's neck in the morning."

"Methinks you should have bedded her and made her forget all about evil spirits lurking about the front gate. Mayhap in doing so, she would have made you forget all about that faery lurking in your head."

“Who? Tania?” Hugh dismissed the comment with what he hoped was a nonchalant tone. “Why would I dwell upon that witch? My life is better without her in it. I know why you think of her fondly. You spent your time under a spell being given all the pleasures of the flesh by her ladies in waiting. I was shackled to a bed and tormented by that spawn of hell.”

“Whatever you need to tell yourself, my lord,” Thomas teased.

“Argh, get to bed.” Hugh stormed past him, suddenly very tired. “And leave me be.”

# Chapter Two

*"Witch!"*

Tania slapped the vision of Lord Bellemare with her hand. Instantly, the whole wall of images disappeared. The faery queen screamed wildly, thrashing about in the air. It was clear now that the earl would never come back to her to keep his promise. The small hope she carried died in that moment. If he denied her to his closest brother, then he would deny her forever. *"Spawn of hell?!"*

Call her a witch, would he? Not worth his time? His life was better without her in it?

Around her the silver walls of the sphere-shaped chamber tarnished, losing their shiny luster. In her need to be away from the divining pool, she blasted up the narrow stairs like a ray of light. Gray sparks shot out of her flesh, hitting the walls and marring the silver finish with rust.

Not knowing where else to go, she went to her great hall, still screaming. Those in her court looked up from their gathering and gasped in unison. Couples stopped dancing, frozen together in the air like statues except for their fluttering wings. The instant the queen took her silver throne, the sweet music of the faeries died and tarnish grew out over her sparkling hall, dimming it and the light with it.

Her subjects looked at her, their wings dropping, the

radiance in their eyes fading with worry. A small burst of light erupted near Tania's throne and Lady Lily, a blonde faery, appeared next to her. Her white wings sparkled with the glittering of stars against her dark blue dress.

"My queen, what has happened?" Lily asked.

Another burst of light erupted and Lily's sister, Roslyn, was on the queen's other side. Roslyn had darker hair. Her translucent dark blue wings matched her sister's dress, just as her sparkling dress of fine silk matched her sister's white wings. Like the entire faery race, the sisters prided themselves on beauty and elegance.

Then why didn't Hugh want her anymore? She was the queen of beauty and elegance!

Tania shook, so angry, so hurt, so desperate to end the pain inside her chest. She wanted to rip out her heart and toss it aside. How could he not love her? How could she still love him?

"My queen?" Roslyn asked, her voice weak.

"Bring me King Lucien," Tania ordered, her words clear as they rang over the quiet hall. The faeries of her court gasped at the command, none moving to obey.

"Nay, not Lucien," Lily begged.

"Not the King of the Damned," Roslyn said. "You do not know what you ask."

"Zanna, Suzette and Rossa are still sick from the last time a demon was brought into this hall." Lily shivered visibly. "Sir Nicholas was merely possessed by one when they took him to their bed. What will happen if you bring the Damned King here?"

Tania didn't move. She didn't want to be reminded of Sir Nicholas. Doing so only reminded her of Hugh.

"Lord Bellemare—" Roslyn didn't finish. Tania's hard look cut her off.

"If you have so much to say, say it to Lucien. Go. Bid him to come to my palace." Tania glanced at Lily. "And you go with her."

"Ah," they gasped, their mouths working as if they would speak. No sound was forthcoming. Weakly, they backed away from the throne. Tania waited, her body tense with the new plan forming in her head. With a sudden burst, the two sisters became small dots of light, zipping out of the great hall.

*I'll teach him the price of breaking his word to a faery,* Tania swore silently. Tears crystallized in her eyes, hardening with her heart. *I'll take him from the one thing that he loves above all others. Bellemare.*

*Fire Palace of the Damned, Kingdom of Hades*

"How was your journey, my sweet little nymph?" King Lucien smiled, twirling a lock of his long black hair around his finger. Dark eyes lifted to meet hers, but the light in his eyes belied any pleasure shown in the expression. Fires burned all around them in his bedchamber—in the oversized fireplace, in basins, on candles and torches. Light strips of gauze hung from the ceiling, fluttering noiselessly around the room. Though the material occasionally blew close to the flames, it did not catch fire. He lounged in a chair before the fireplace. The orange light cast his face with a ghoulish ferocity.

Mia didn't move from her place in the doorway, as she stared at Lucien. He had many pet names for her, but "sweet nymph" was one of his favorites. "My slave" was more appropriate. She was his, bound to him until he let her go. There was only one way out of Lucien's control and that was by death. But, even then, her soul would be his, burning eternally, there to be brought back again and again. So what was better? Living as his slave or burning as a kept soul?

His gaze flickered over her, dispassionate and hard before traveling back to stare into her eyes. Mia waited, knowing something was coming.

"How are things in the mortal realm?" he asked.

The practically nonexistent dress he'd put on her that morning was fashioned of torn material. Suddenly, it disappeared, only to be instantaneously replaced with the mortal servant gown she'd stolen and changed into at Bellemare Castle. His dressing her in the gown wasn't necessary, for in his eyes she read the knowledge of her betrayal.

Her stomach knotted and tears entered her eyes. She tried to hold them back, aware that he would get strength from her fear and pain. Mia had only gone to Bellemare to warn the family, to shake them up with talk of the devil so they'd be on guard against whatever Lucien had planned. Mia didn't know how, but Lucien became stronger each passing day and with that strength he grew bolder. She feared that one day soon he'd find a way to cross over into the realm of mortals. If that happened, the humans would be doomed. Lucien's army of demons would take over and wherever that army marched, death and destruction lay in its wake.

"Do you really believe that in betraying me, you will redeem any part of you? You are damned, my sweet Mia. Damned. Do you think any good deed can relinquish the blackness that is even now eating your soul?"

"How did you know where I was?" Mia tried to keep her voice level. She had been so careful when she followed his demon through the portal. The creature didn't see her, didn't see anything beyond his gruesome task.

"Mia, tsk, tsk," Lucien scolded, almost naked, except for a pair of breeches. It was his normal attire when in the Fire Palace. His bare toes curled and stretched, as if an extension of his bored tone. Mia wasn't put at ease by his manners. Lucien was the most dangerous when he appeared disinterested. "Do you think me so blinded by your pretty face? Did you think by pleasuring me as you did, I would not know the true purpose in your submission? Did you think I believed your final surrender to me was real? That you had finally given in to me completely? Did you think I wouldn't know the truth? I am the king of lies and deceit, Mia."

His eyes stayed on hers, holding her gaze. Lucien lifted his hand, palm out, toward the bed. Flames erupted on the dark fur coverlet, growing into the shape of two figures caught up in indescribable acts of passion. Lucien had the power to control the fire and had shown her many things in the flames, horrible things she wished to forget. Most times she didn't know what was real and what was from his imagination. He claimed he merely watched the cruel actions of others with the flames—rapes, murders, those filthy little secrets mortals kept.

Mia didn't need to be told who the flames represented this time. She saw well the chain links she'd worn for him, heard the memory of her cries echoing in her brain, telling him she loved him. Each cry was like a knife to her heart.

*I love you, Lucien, I love only you.*

"Cease." She turned her eyes to him. "I tire of this, Lucien."

"If only that were true, sweet nymph." Orange light danced along his muscular chest, glowing in his wicked eyes. Even now she desired him. The side of his mouth curled, as if he knew exactly what she thought. His hips rocked suggestively in his seat and she couldn't help but see the stiff outline of his erection beneath the tight black pants.

*Say it,* his voice echoed from the flames on the bed.

"If you are to kill me," she whispered, not feeling as brave as she would have liked, "then kill me."

*I love you,* her past self answered in the throes of passion, giving in to him. The words echoed inside her, gnawing at her but not killing her. The pain grew in her chest and she wanted to cry out, strike his face until he could no longer look at her, smile at her, make her ache for him.

Mia's eyes were drawn back to the bed, to see her shame enacted in fire. It was her curse, the unbearable passion she found in his arms. Some days she just wished he'd let her die, take the second half of her soul and be done with it.

"Did you think I would not know?" he asked.

She forced her feet to step inside the room, hardening herself to his cruel taunting. "Save your show for someone whose soul can actually be affected by it."

She was instantly sorry for the words. Taunting the king of all demons was not a wise course to take.

Lucien grinned and fisted his hand. The flames on the bed instantly smothered as if they'd never been there. Just as quickly, he disappeared. Mia stiffened to feel him standing directly behind her. She didn't turn to look at him, not daring to move. The chamber was hot, but the heat never bothered him. In fact, he claimed to welcome it as the fire warmed his otherwise chilled skin. Mia wasn't so immune. She started to sweat beneath the thick mortal clothing.

"What's the matter, sweet nymph?" he spat. "Hot?"

Mia didn't look at him as she stared at the dark gray stone of the castle wall.

"I asked if you were hot," he yelled in her ear, causing her to struggle for breath at the sudden demonic sound. The demon within him had entered his voice, evident in the gravelly harsh tone.

"Aye," she whispered, nodding fearfully. She could deal with Lucien when he was calm, but when he called out his inner demon it was another situation altogether. She knew the cruel acts the demon was capable of.

Or perchance there was no inner demon in him. Mayhap he was all demon and she just needed to think it was a dark creature inside the man—a man she could love, could tell herself it was all right to care for. But, perhaps she only lied to herself and any trace of the man Lucien had once been was truly gone—if he'd ever been a man.

Nay, she couldn't think like that. There had to be something left in him, something she caught glimpses of in his eyes, something worth caring for. It was the only way she could stand her existence.

As far as she understood, King Lucien started as a non-demonic being. It was the way magic worked. Just like King Ean was an elf before being King of the Blessed, as was Merrick before being Unblessed, Lucien had to be something. The pure demon who controlled Lucien, the one who put him to rule, could not exist in either realm, or even on the earth. It was a thing, a nothingness, pure evil feeding on emotions and dark deeds that would forever burn. Mayhap it couldn't even be called a demon, for it was the darkest magic. Understanding made it more difficult for her to hate him.

"Was that so hard?" The demonic voice crackled with each breath. A long time had passed since the evil within was so noticeably close to the surface. Lucien walked around her. The black in his eyes spread, filling in the whites. Two tiny red dots replaced his pupils and his hard face looked like marble dusted with ash as he stood uncomfortably close. Suddenly, the servant's gown disappeared from her body, leaving her naked and vulnerable. "Better?"

"Aye," she nodded, though in truth she almost preferred the human clothes to such exposure.

His breath left him in a long, ugly hiss. "I give you things none other has. I give you a place in my palace as my mistress. You are worshiped by demons, respected and feared by them. I let you keep half of your soul so that you may still feel something besides death and this is how you repay my generosity?" His tone was soft, growing by small degrees as he spoke. Lucien flung his hand toward the bed, lighting it anew with the flames to mimic the passion shared the night before. "With this treachery!" He swung his hand to the side, moving the flames from the bed to the floor with a resounding whoosh, forming two fiery figures. It was William, the mortal wizard, standing with her as they had in Bellemare's great hall. William's figure crumpled as she'd blown magic into his face. She'd stolen the slight power from Lucien. Then her image kneeled, kissing William's mortal lips to make him fall unconscious.

Lucien sucked the flames back into himself, holding the fire in his palm. Black smoke curled over them, forming a dark cloud along the ceiling of his bedchamber. Mia didn't dare speak. The fire wound around his arm and neck like a snake, before rolling in a ball toward his hand. It twisted into the shape of a dagger and solidified to become a real blade. He wielded it before her, touching her lips with the hot steel.

"You dare to kiss another with this mouth?" he demanded, his tone sinister. The flames sparked in his eyes. "You think you can cause me pain by betraying me? Do you think you can teach me anything about suffering? I am the king of evil. You cannot teach me anything I do not already know."

"Luc—" She foolishly tried to speak.

The knife tip dug into her lip, drawing blood. He wanted to stab her, she could see it in his eyes, felt it in whatever soul she had left. He drew the blade back. Mia flinched, not trying to run. Why should she? He could come after her, catch her wherever she went. Even if she was to escape, with half her soul intact, he would have the other half and with it he'd have the means to capture her. With it, he'd call to her, make her delirious to come back even when she knew she shouldn't. She shivered, hating him for what he was capable of and unsure as to how to stop him.

"Leave the mortals be," she pleaded, knowing it could very well be the last thing she said to him. "Let Bellemare have its blessing. With such a corrupt mortal world, why do you need the Bellemare family?"

"You know the reason, Mia." Lucien took the blade, swinging it around in his hand. The demon burned bright in his black eyes. "I need those souls if I am to become more powerful. The blessed always have the farthest to fall."

"You do not need more power," she said softly, hoping to calm him. Shaking, she lifted her hand, moving her lips closer to his. The taste of blood was in her mouth, salty and thick. "You are powerful enough."

Lucien jerked away, lifting the blade higher. "Do you think you can tempt me with lips that touched another? Do you think you can do anything I will not know about? I should cut your lips from you, you treacherous whore."

She whimpered as the knife slashed the air. Instead of hitting her, Lucien drove the blade into his own stomach. He gasped, blood trickling from his lips down his chin and throat. It splattered from his wound, over her cheeks and neck in hot beads. He left the weapon imbedded in his flesh and grabbed her face. Kissing her with his bloody mouth, he grunted with each movement of his body. She knew he felt the pain of what he had done.

His lips close to hers, he said, "Do you think I will hesitate to do the same to you if you betray me again?"

Tears ran down her cheeks and she shook her head in denial. He could stab her a thousand times and bring her back after each and every one. The salty taste of his blood was in her mouth, stinging her with the potency of it. She knew he could kill her if he so chose, and knew that only her hate of him held him back. Her hate fed his powers and he liked making her fall to his will again and again.

"I can give you everything or I can take it all away. The choice is yours, Mia. Believe me when I say, death is not the worst I am capable of." Lucien snarled at her, disappearing from the chamber.

Seconds after he left, manacles wrapped her wrists and ankles. Chains pulled her to the floor with their impossibly heavy weight, leading to the poster of his bed. Unable to move, she lay naked on the floor, watching the flames of the fireplace. The demon blood in her mouth burned and she tried to spit it out. It did no good. Nothing would ever get rid of Lucien's taste. The Damned King's scent marred her completely and she knew it was only a matter of time before she was utterly his.

Lucien stormed down the hall, holding his fiery hands out to the side to make the dark gray stone of his castle walls light with his rage. The roaring flames locked Mia even more securely in his bedchamber. Tapestries burned, curling and falling around him as he destroyed everything of beauty around him. Lucien didn't care. He could fix it later if he wished. Right now, he didn't want to be reminded of beauty's treacherous face, her easy lies.

Forming a ball of flames in his hand, he tossed it back and forth between his palms as he entered the great hall of his palace. Thin columns reached up to the ceiling, the black stone roughly cut with sharp jagged edges. The ceilings were tall, but like the rest of his palace, they were subject to his whims. Right now stone spikes grew down, giant stalactites with deadly points.

A large bonfire burned in the middle of the hall, casting light over the dark, shiny stone, giving depth where shadows liked to creep. The fire was held in place by a giant circular pit in the ground. The edges of the floor lifted up slightly around the flames, as if the stone had been rolled over to make the fiery centerpiece.

Holding his flaming hand higher, Lucien looked around for a moving target. His hall was empty. There was no one to pelt with his wrath.

The Damned King growled, motioning his hand upward. A stone head grew from the dark floor, creaking and moaning as it came to be. Lucien paced around it, glaring at each line he'd created until he stood before a life size Mia. Roaring with anger he threw the flames at the statue, repeatedly hitting it until the stone crumpled under the immense heat, and still he threw more, weakening himself as the rage boiled on.

"Ah!" A tiny gasp penetrated his brain.

Lucien turned, his fiery hand held back, knowing the demon he carried was enjoying himself immensely. He caught his reflection in the polished black column. His skin had turned to an ashen gray, scorched like the last embers of a fire. His eyes were black pits streaked with the crimson of blood and hate. Seeing a speck of white light in the dark bowels of his hall, he parted his lips to expose a mouthful of fangs.

*"Ahh!"* The tiny faery screamed, reaching to grab another faery light behind it. The second speck fought with the first as if each trying to push the other forward.

"What are you doing in my hall?" Lucien growled, breathing heavily through his nose so each breath was a snort of irritation.

*"Qu-queen..."* a small voice stuttered.

"Speak up," Lucien yelled. Fire spurted over his entire being, only to puff out with a gust of smoke.

The two faeries flew closer, weaving as if uncertain before forming to their taller heights before him. They held each other looking fearfully at his chest.

"You are, ah, King Lucien..." The dark-haired one pointed at his chest. "Ah...?"

The blade he'd stuck in himself was still there. He grabbed it, pulling it out. Blood ran down his stomach. Smiling cruelly, he fed off their fear of him as he brought the blade to his lips. Lucien licked the blade, watching them closely for a reaction. A rush of strength came over him as they grabbed each other tighter.

"Queen Tania wishes for you to..." the lighter faery said in a hurry as if trying to force the words out before she lost her voice altogether. Her wings drooped toward the ground.

"To come," the darker one added.

"To Feia," the blonde finished.

Queen Tania requested an audience with him? Lucien laughed, tilting back his head as the dark sound echoed off the barren walls. Did the queen really think she could stop him from sending his demons into Bellemare? Did she think she would be safe to confront him on her own ground? Did a faery really believe she could best the king of all that was damned?

"I accept," Lucien answered, eager to have an excuse to leave the Fire Palace. He tossed the blade at the two faeries. They screamed and huddled close together as it came for them. The blade disappeared into a puff of smoke inches before hitting them. They yelped and made popping noises as they became little dots of light. Still laughing, Lucien bowed and disappeared, leaving the hysterical women to fly frantically out of his hall.

"What do you mean William is gone?" Hugh demanded, slamming his fist on a nearby dining table. He stood before the fireplace, having thoroughly checked the abovestairs chambers himself. The earl turned his gaze to where his knight, Sir Geoffrey, awaited his orders. Aside from Thomas and Geoffrey, there were only a few of his most loyal guards in the hall.

"We have looked everywhere, my lord." Geoffrey gave him a meaningful look. Hugh trusted the man with his life. They'd fought in many skirmishes together and had even trained for knighthood as children under the same lord.

"None have passed by the castle gate," Euric offered, stepping forward. He was in charge of the front gate. "And we have checked the surrounding wall. There is naught to draw suspicion. Even if someone could survive the fall, they would leave a trail. There is naught to make us suspect William was there. If he is gone, William did not leave that way."

Hugh closed his eyes. He should have followed his instincts and looked for William the night before, but they'd been so sure he was merely sleeping with the maid. Directing his attention back to Geoffrey, he asked, "And the woman?"

Geoffrey shook his head. "None know of a maid with eyes like you describe. Are you sure you—?"

Hugh's hard look stopped him from finishing the inquiry.

"Forgive me, my lord," Geoffrey said. "I did not mean to question you."

Hugh nodded absently. Knowing it was hopeless even as he gave the order, he said, "Search again."

"Aye," Geoffrey nodded. He waved his hand at the awaiting guards as he strode toward the stairwell leading out of the castle. "Euric, you search the wall again and get men on the outside of the castle."

"Aye," said Euric.

"Tobias, get five men and search every inch of this castle," Geoffrey continued. "And gather the servants. Look for a woman with violet eyes. She has to be here somewhere. Tell the others."

The sound of their footsteps lightened and Hugh looked at his brother. He trusted Geoffrey to do what must be done and resisted the urge to go look himself. Besides, his gut now told him that William was no longer in the mortal realm.

"They took him," Hugh said.

"Who?" Thomas frowned.

"They, them, the magic creatures!" Hugh exclaimed. "Who else?"

"William is gone, my lord," Rees appeared, bowing as he stood atop a table. "We have looked all over the castle. There is no sign of him or his magic. None of us sensed him casting spells."

That confirmed it. If the magical creatures of Bellemare couldn't find him, then William must truly be lost.

"There is something else though, my lord." Another

creature appeared on the floor. It was Giles, the household brownie. He stumbled drunkenly. The creature spent too much time in the pantry floating in the barrels of ale and mead.

"What?" Hugh demanded.

"Ah!" Rees disappeared off the table only to appear on the floor by Giles. The brownie blinked as Rees stood before him in aggression. "I'm in charge here. You tell me and I will tell Lord Bellemare."

"Rees!" Hugh interrupted. He didn't have time for their arguing. Not now. "Giles, what else?"

Giles burped and scratched his head. "I cannot remember."

"Argh," Hugh made a move to squash the troublesome brownie. Thomas grabbed his arm, stopping him.

"Giles, what do you know of our brother, William?" Thomas asked.

"Ah, aye, William. Methinks he's passed," Giles said.

"Dead," Hugh whispered, stricken with a severe pain in his chest.

"Well, uh," Giles frowned, lifting his finger. He never got a chance to explain as a shout sounded over the hall.

"Lord Bellemare! Come at once!" It was Euric yelling up the stairwell. "A foal!"

"Nay, my lord! Not dead!" Giles yelled. "Passed through. William passed through."

Hugh was too tense to feel much relief at the brownie's words. He ran for the courtyard with Thomas on his heels. His sword hung along his waist, ready to be drawn should the need arise. He had a sick feeling in the pit of his stomach that it would.

✧

"I like the changes you have made to your palace," Lucien said as he walked into the tarnished faery hall.

Tania lifted her head to look at the Damned King from her throne. He moved leisurely, glancing around as if appreciating the dark atmosphere. She knew the second he'd appeared and had left the way open so he could find entry.

It had been a long time since she'd seen Lucien and part of her trembled to have openly invited him to be in her home, but a greater part of her ached, demanding that she do it. He was the only one strong enough to bring Hugh back to Feia and make him answer for leaving her.

"Your demons grow bold," Tania said.

"Are you blaming your new look on my demons?" Lucien asked. His tanned flesh was splotched with ashen spots. He looked sickly, but she wasn't fooled by the pallor of his features. Threading his hands behind his back, he strolled around the empty great hall floor. Her faeries had left her, unsure what their queen was thinking but not willing to wait around for the King of the Damned to show himself in their court. "I assure you, they rarely leave a castle standing, should they take it to mind to refashion it."

"They cross into the mortal realm all too freely," Tania said, ignoring his sinister teasing.

"Ah, that." Lucien bowed, a mocking gesture. "Forgive my rudeness. I forgot to thank you for lowering your magical guard so that they may pass more easily."

"Can you cross?" Tania asked, not returning his smile.

Lucien's expression didn't change, but he also didn't answer. Tania concluded by his silence that he could not.

"Pity," she lied.

"Now you have really piqued my curiosity." Lucien leisurely climbed the stairs to stand by her throne. Stopping next to her, he reached down to touch her face. "The hall is not the only thing that has changed, is it? What has happened to the beautiful faery queen? Surely the horrors of war have not touched you so deeply as to cause this." The edge of his fingernail traced a black line along her cheek. The feel of it burned her flesh, just enough to sting but not cause damage. "Why do you ask me here? What has happened that you should join me?"

"I'm not joining you," Tania said.

Lucien laughed. "You already have, little faery. Whatever malady you suffer has made you join me. I can sense the darkness in you, the hate, so close to my own magic. Mmm, it is delightful."

Tania closed her eyes, deliberately pulling her face from his hand. Lucien walked behind her, circling her chair before standing directly in front of her. Placing his hands on the arms of her throne, he leaned over her, trapping her to the seat. Tania felt a shiver of fear work up her spine at his nearness. Heat radiated off him, but that wasn't all. His very presence crushed whatever pleasure or hope she had left, depressing her more. Lucien was like an empty void that sucked and drained everything around him. Normally, he couldn't hurt her, but she was weakened from a broken heart and his nearness easily influenced her emotions.

The Damned King licked his lips. Closing his eyes, he slowly turned his head to the side, smelling her. When he'd finished, he said, "Methought you had been damaged, my virgin queen, but I now see that it is being undamaged that haunts you. I smell your heart. It aches, each little broken piece of it."

He sighed heavily, a faint smile on his lips. "Each piece calls to me for help. Your soul wants me to be here and a part of you longs for me to end your suffering."

Tania closed her eyes. To have him speak of it sullied the emotions she felt.

"Who do I owe thanks for this change in you?" Lucien touched her thigh, rubbing it through the thin silk of her gown. "Who would you have me punish to free you from this? Just say the words. Ask me to help you, to take away your pain. Give it to me and I will give you such pleasures in return."

"I'm not asking you for that. You cannot have my soul," she answered, just as softly. "I will never give it to you."

He drew his finger along the inside of her leg, sending heat wherever he touched. His tone low, his words measured, he continued seductively, "Then perhaps you will give me something else? Keep your soul, but give in to me, join me and I will give you the same pleasure. Even you can admit the generosity of that offer, can you not, my queen?"

Tania tensed. The "something else" he wanted was clear. Her body responded to his impious words, his unthinkable offer. Lust wasn't necessarily a sin, but lust the way he offered it was. There would only be malice in his kisses, evil in his touch, death in his love. Funny to think the King of the Damned could feel something like love, but love was like all emotions—dark and light, blessed and unblessed, happy and sad. It was where that love came from that made it good or evil.

"Shall I repay this mystery man of yours by showing you how wickedly enjoyable it is to fall from faery grace? Shall I bind you to me, to the pleasure of sin? Would you like me to take that ache away from you? I have the power. I can take your suffering, give you sin without remorse, give you pleasure without consequence. Think of the freedom, the power, the pleasure."

Tania gasped, breathing hard. His offer was tempting. Why had she called him here? What insanity had taken hold in her to make her think she could fight Lucien and win? She was too weak. He was so strong.

Taking his hand in hers, she pushed it away. "Are you finished?"

"Do you reject my proposal, little faery?"

"You call that a proposal?" It took all her power to deny him.

"You wish for me to explain in full, torrid detail what I am proposing?" His tone dipped so low she could barely hear it.

"I wish for you to stop talking so we may discuss the reason I asked you here."

Lucien laughed and pushed directly back from her throne. A chair formed behind him, catching him so he didn't fall on the floor. He sat, facing her, his eyes on her—studying, probing, mocking. The dark and twisted lines of his throne were not her doing. She knew his magic to be much stronger than hers, but he shouldn't have been able to manipulate her palace. This was her home, built by her magic.

"I'm listening." He lazily draped his arms over the sides, tapping his nails in a steady rhythm against the stone chair.

"Lord Bellemare," Tania said, doing her best to regain her composure. "I want him brought to me. Alive."

Lucien froze, his hands lifted in mid-tap as he studied her for a long moment. She'd shocked him.

"In exchange," she continued, "I will grant you one night in the mortal realm. I will let the magic of the faeries slip away so you may pass through one of our rings."

"Not much can be done in one night," Lucien said.

"It is a simple task I ask, but one I cannot do myself for reasons I will not discuss." Tania arched a brow. "And one night is more than you have now."

Lucien grinned, lifting his hand to the side. A small ring of fire appeared in his palm. "Is that all?"

"The Bellemare family remains unharmed."

"Mmm, nay," Lucien shook his head. "I cannot promise that. No fun is to be had in that pledge."

"Then his family is to remain unharmed for a fortnight after he is brought to me alive. Naught can happen to them before that time. Not one single injury by your doing or responsibility."

He merely stared at her.

"Have we a deal?" It took all her willpower to stay calm. Lucien was not a man to easily cross.

"Why?"

"That is my concern." She lifted her chin. "Have we a deal?"

"Is he the one?"

"Have we a deal?"

"Kidnapping protected mortals is a grave thing," he warned, though his concern was fake. "You would not want anyone to know, would you?"

The fire twisted off the tips of his hand, moving through the air toward her chin. He wiggled his fingers, sending the fiery trail down her chest. The flame glanced over her nipples, igniting a shockwave of carnal pleasure over her. She slashed her hand through the flame, freezing it so he was forced to stop. The fire trail dropped, crashing on the ground like tinkling red-orange gems before puffing into a line of smoke.

"What would happen if King Ean found out?" he continued as if nothing had happened. "Bellemare is blessed by him after all. You have seen what happens to people who take his wards.

King Merrick stole Juliana and the two kingdoms are now at war. Are the faeries ready to fight Tegwen as well? Will you join forces with Merrick? Will you join forces with me?"

"You know as well as I, to do that would only help you. I will not join you, Lucien, and I will not cross King Ean. My business with Lord Bellemare is my own and my taking him does not concern the Blessed Kingdom. Why do you think I send you to fetch him? The deed of crossing him over will be yours. Now, I ask you again? Have we a deal?" Tania was apprehensive, as she waited his answer.

"Aye," Lucien agreed, nodding. "We do."

"When?"

"It is already in motion." He grinned. "I will simply change my course for yours instead."

Holding out his hand, fire formed in his palm, molding into a knife. He took the blade and slashed it across his palm before offering the hilt to Tania. She hesitated. He wanted the agreement in blood? She had thought he'd want to leave himself an out, but a contract like this was impenetrable. Knowing that he'd be bound to bring Hugh to her alive and to keep his family safe for at least a short while after, she held out her hand. A few weeks would give her enough time to set things right with Hugh.

Instead of taking the knife, Tania stretched her fingers and waited. She didn't have the stomach to cut herself. Lucien laughed, even as he sliced through her hand.

Tania moaned at the sharp pain. Faeries weren't meant for ugly dealings such as these. They were meant to only see beauty and happiness. Each moment that passed a piece of her died, withering with Lucien's nearness. She only hoped he brought Hugh to her in time to save whatever light magic she had left. Only, when Hugh was brought to her, what would she do? Force him to love her?

*I will deal with that when the time comes.*

Lucien pressed his hand to hers, his blood burned like acid as it bound into her system. She screamed, automatically jerking her arm away. He held it tighter, refusing to let go.

"So shall it be," he said, his black eyes bright with an inner fire. "A pact is made and bound by blood."

Tania felt nauseous, even as she nodded, whispering, "So shall it be."

Lucien disappeared, taking his throne chair with him and Tania fell forward, landing on her hands and knees as she threw up onto the ground. Her body burned and the knife wound refused to heal itself. She was getting weaker. She hadn't much time.

Whimpering, she rolled on her side and curled into a ball at the foot of her throne. She felt Lucien's influence all around her. "Please let this alliance not be a mistake. Make Hugh love me again. Make him love me."

# Chapter Three

Euric's face was white when Hugh and Thomas reached the courtyard. Without uttering a word, the man pointed toward Bellemare's stables. A crowd of servants and knights had gathered outside the wooden structure. Hugh pushed through them. A woman screamed near the front of the group, drawing his attention briefly to her. He couldn't see any reason for her cries so dismissed her as hysterical as he continued his way through the crowd.

"Back away!" Geoffrey yelled. The crowd listened, albeit slowly.

"What is...?" Thomas' words trailed off.

Hugh came out of the crowd, his stomach tight with worry that it was William. The relief he felt was bittersweet as he looked down. A dead foal lay on the ground, its head missing and its body still covered in the evidence of its birth. Behind him, he heard the low tones of the castle's monk reciting prayers. Hugh was too shaken to translate the Latin words in his head.

"What did this?" Thomas asked, kneeling by the dead animal to examine it closely without touching it. "The neck looks gnawed on."

"That is not from the ones stillborn last night," Hugh answered. "The markings on his legs are different."

"You mean we lost another?" Thomas swore softly. "Nay, it cannot be. Why is this happening?"

Hugh glanced at his brother, thankful that he'd said the words softly. He didn't want the people of Bellemare panicking any more than they were. A loud thump sounded inside the stables causing a collective gasp of alarm.

"What was that?" Thomas stood. Hugh looked at the stables, trying to listen over the murmur of voices behind him.

Another thump sounded, followed by a crash against the stable wall. The wood reverberated, sending chills over Hugh. Require him to face a man three times his size in battle and he would do so without question, but this? He swallowed, drawing his sword. The action prompted the others to do the same. He vaguely heard the monk urging the crowd further back still, frightening them with words about the evil that lurked within the stables.

"Mayhap the monk and the violet-eyed woman are right," Hugh said to Thomas. "Mayhap the devil has come to Bellemare."

"Aye," Thomas agreed. Geoffrey gave the brothers a strange look but said nothing.

Someone passed Hugh a torch and he took it, holding it up in one hand while wielding his sword with the other. He went forward first, leading the way into the dark stables. More evidence of slaughtered horses greeted them and the acrid smell of blood was thick on the air. A horse whinnied and stomped, kicking at the wood, giving evidence to the sound they'd heard outside.

"Show yourself," Hugh ordered, holding the torch high. His skin prickled with the knowledge that they weren't alone, that something else was in the room with them, waiting in the darkness. He stepped over an unrecognizable bloody mass on the floor, doing his best not to breathe in the smell.

They passed a mare still tethered in her stall. Thomas patted the animal's neck, looking alongside it. He shook his head, indicating that no one was there.

"This is Lord Bellemare," Hugh shouted, "show yourself!"

"Do you really think a man did this?" Geoffrey asked. "Perchance a wolf?"

Suddenly, a low growl came from the back. It was a throaty, juicy sound. Hugh edged forward, concentrating on his surroundings. The circle of light did little to give comfort in the darkness. Something flew out of the shadows at him, hitting his wrist and forcing him to drop the torch. As the light fell, he realized it was a severed horse's leg that struck him.

*Aye, perchance a wolf,* Hugh thought, hoping it was so, but not convinced by the explanation. The torch fire hit straw and ignited, sending a blaze to light the stables.

"By all that is holy!" Thomas pointed at the beast that had attacked the horses. It wasn't an animal, and most definitely not a wolf. "It looks like a—a man."

"That is not a man," Geoffrey whispered. "It is a..."

"A man-beast," Hugh finished, unable to think of what else to call it.

The creature wore the tattered clothes of a nobleman, covered in dirt and leaves. Skeletal hands reached out, dripping with blood. Flesh rotted off the dead man's face, hanging in patches.

The earl gagged, Geoffrey made a weak noise and Thomas swore under his breath. Hugh knew they were all three frightened, but he trusted the other two to stay by him.

They had all seen dead men after the bodies had been left out past their time for burial. They had seen corpses and horror, slain men on the sides of battlefields. Such was the lot of a knight. But, never had they seen a man come back from the dead.

"Lord Eadward?" Hugh whispered, seeing the crest on the creature's cloak. The symbol was as familiar to him as his own crest. Eadward was Juliana's dead fiancé and had been a friend of Hugh's father. The man had been killed by his demon-possessed son, who also happened to be their childhood friend—Sir Nicholas. It took place right before Juliana was taken by Merrick to the Otherworld.

"It cannot be," Geoffrey said. "Lord Eadward has been dead for nigh over a year."

The fire spread, heating the structure. Hugh kept his eyes forward, ordering the others, "We need to save the horses. These are the best of Bellemare's stock. We cannot lose them."

They slowly backed away, keeping their eyes on the creature. Hugh shivered. Should they confront it? Or did they save the horses and run away? If they chose to fight the beast, how could he kill a dead man? And how could they run away with such a beast on the loose?

Eadward opened his mouth, gurgling. It was an awful sound, one the man would never have made in his living years. Or was it wrong to think of the creature as Eadward? Hugh's mind raced, trying to grasp what he was seeing. He knew the possibility of such things as this could exist, but that didn't make witnessing it any easier to believe.

Hugh wondered how the creature could see them without eyes, but the face turned as if it knew exactly where the men were. Suddenly, Eadward lunged, baring unholy fangs as he flew through the air with predatory ease, taking them by surprise. Hugh automatically lifted his sword to fight, the motion a reflex from years of training.

The blade slid into Eadward's stomach, but the man-beast didn't stop coming. Bony fingers bit into Hugh's shoulders seconds before Eadward's teeth sunk into his neck.

"Ahh," Hugh yelled, pushing the hilt of his sword forward to get the dead man off of him. But Eadward possessed a strength in death that he never had in life as he latched himself into Hugh's flesh.

"Hugh!" Thomas cried.

"Kill him," Hugh yelled, desperate to have the creature off as he was brought to his knees. The blade stuck out of the creature's back, having run him through to no consequence. Hugh pushed at the bony chest with his free hand as the hilt of his sword pressed into his stomach. His wrist twisted as his sword hand was trapped at an odd angle. Eadward pinned him to the ground, feeling five times heavier than he could've possibly weighed.

"Pull him off," Geoffrey hollered. Hugh's body jerked as they tried to free him from the man-beast's hold. Eadward gripped him tighter. "Get the head!"

"Stand back," Thomas ordered.

Hugh's vision swam and bright spots of light made it hard to see. The fire danced all around him, heating his flesh as the stables continued to burn. Weakly, he mumbled, "Save the horses. They are the best of the stock."

Thomas didn't appear to hear him. The sound of footsteps and yelling ensued behind his head and he knew his men had come to fight the fire. In the chaos, he saw Thomas above him, his sword drawn, his face tight as he swung the blade down. Hugh closed his eyes, his body braced—braced for hope of liberation from his pain, braced in fear that the strike wouldn't come fast enough. Water doused his head as more shouts sounded. Thomas screamed. Eadward's body jerked off of Hugh, releasing the pressure on his stomach, but the creature's gnawing head was still in place. Then, a fiery heat cut through his arm as Thomas didn't stop the swing of the blade in time.

Dizzy, Hugh opened his eyes to see Geoffrey pulling Eadward's head from his neck only to toss it into the flames. He heard the horses being led to safety, or was that pounding his own heart in his ears? He couldn't be sure.

"Blessed Saints, Hugh," Thomas said at his side, trying to hold the wound on Hugh's arm as he dragged his brother out of the burning stables into daylight.

Hugh tried to answer, but it was too hard. Though he could hear, he couldn't speak, couldn't see what was happening around him.

"Easy, brother," Thomas said, his voice strained, "remain with us."

William moaned before taking long, deep breaths as he opened one eye. The chamber was dark and quiet, and an uneven surface jabbed against his back, uncomfortable but not unbearable. His body felt heavy, pulled, and it took a moment before he realized he hung from chains along a damp stone wall.

A prisoner? But whose?

His first thought was the giant, Lord Angus. While he slept, William dreamt of the giant's daughter, his mind stuck in a continuous loop of memory as their time together started and ended only to start again. As far as dreams went, it wasn't a horrific one for he had found pleasure in her arms, though their time together didn't end well. Lord Angus hadn't been happy to discover the tryst.

Did Angus find him and take him prisoner? Without light, it was impossible to tell where he was. He could very well be in a giant's dungeon or in a farfadet's. His feet touched the floor, but that wasn't a clue. Aside from the darkness and the chains, his senses were almost completely deprived of any outside stimulation. All was quiet, except when he moved.

It took some concentrating, but he remembered seeing the woman with violet eyes at Bellemare. She'd been magical, of that he was sure. A magical mercenary sent to the mortal realm to bring him to justice? By the feelings in his limbs, the tingling knowledge that magic surrounded him, he knew he'd been brought back to the immortal realm.

"Light. I need light," he said to himself, racking his brain for the right spell to use. William struggled with his chains, but they were too secure. He doubted mere strength would free him of them. Looking around, he couldn't see anything in the pitch black. He sighed heavily and called out, "Ho! Does anyone there remember the spell to make light?"

Thomas paced outside his brother's bedchamber. Even though it was daylight outside, the hall was dim. The faint sound of a bell ringing followed by Hugh's weak cough made him stop his pacing so he could lean his head against the door. The physician had shooed him from the room as he worked applying herbs, burning incense and placing holy relics along the chamber to incite a recovery.

William was gone, completely disappeared. Word of Hugh's illness had spread, inciting a panic within the population of

Bellemare. Charms were carried and placed through the castle and grounds. The small chapel was filled daily and the monk was up at all hours blessing the castle and pleading for deliverance against the wickedness that plagued them.

It had taken some doing, but Thomas finally convinced the monk that a crazed peasant had attacked Hugh and not an evil spirit. The stables had burned and any evidence to the contrary was hidden within the ashes. Though they managed to save the horses, many of the animals were ill from breathing smoke and a few were scarred by the fire. A couple of the stallions had been struck by fiery thatch from the stable roof and were in much pain. Killing horses was never a pleasant task but it was one that had to be done. Luckily, Geoffrey had taken care of the nasty business for him. Another one of the mares had lost her foal, leaving only one pregnant horse. Guards sat by the animal's side day and night to protect her. She was one of the last to get pregnant and it would be awhile until she delivered.

At times, Thomas would almost convince himself that it hadn't been Lord Eadward back from the dead, but then he'd see Sir Geoffrey's face and he'd know. Geoffrey was certain that William had been eaten by the creature that attacked Hugh. With little choice, Thomas brought Geoffrey into confidence, introducing him to the magical tenants of the castle. He only hoped the man recovered from the shock. The last time Thomas saw him, he still looked pale and shaken.

Rees refused to leave Hugh's side, though Thomas did have to warn the spright about interfering with the physician's work. The doctor came at a high price, but Thomas did what he must for the life of his brother. He'd sell everything they owned to save Hugh.

Until he knew Hugh's fate, he didn't feel right leaving to search for William, but the longer he waited the more he feared for William's life. Already he had the magical creatures trying to figure out a way to get him to the Otherworld. Heinic claimed he could brew a potion but it had been a long time since he'd done so. If there was a chance his youngest brother was alive, Thomas swore he would find a way to bring him home.

Once, a year ago, when they'd asked how to get from one realm to the other so they could come home, King Merrick had told them, "Your journey begins as any other, by walking out the front gate of the castle." Easy for the King of the Unblessed to say, he had magical powers. Thomas had ridden out his front gate many times and only once did he ride into the Otherworld—and that was with William's help.

Thomas heard footsteps and pulled back from where he listened. Moments later, the door was opened and the physician came out. The man carried a bowl filled with blood.

"I have done all I could," the physician said. "The wound on his neck and arm have been cauterized and I have bled as much poison as I could from his body."

"Poison?" Thomas frowned.

"The poisons of the body. It is what causes the earl to be sick," the physician explained, "though I would not doubt that some grave toxin seeped into his body from the injury. There are leeches on his chest above his heart. They should remain until the morrow. Then, take them off and throw them immediately into an old fire. Once the fire burns out, take the ash and bury it."

Thomas nodded, noting the instructions.

"I must warn you." The physician lowered his voice. "Even if the earl does heal, there is a chance he will have caught whatever madness possessed the man that bit him. I can tell by the wound that the man had sharpened teeth, not a good sign, perhaps a sign of witchery. Maladies of the mind are easily spread through bites and this one was so close to the earl's head. We can only hope the madness did not travel up, but down to his foot or hand. Then he will only shake in the limbs from time to time but be of sound mind. If it goes the other way, I fear the worst."

"Many thanks." Thomas stepped back, letting the man take the tainted bowl of blood past.

Though the chamber was stifling hot when he entered, Thomas didn't dare risk Hugh's health by putting out the fire. The earl's room was a large square, with the fireplace and a huge bed stuffed with straw and lined with feathers for softness. A large fur rug covered most of the stone floor. Hugh had a writing table, complete with parchments and wax. The family crest hung on one wall, matching the ring on Hugh's finger. Pulling a red, padded chair next to Hugh's bed, Thomas sat.

A faint odor was in the air, the smell of burnt flesh and incense. Hugh's chest was uncovered and two black leeches sucked from him. Thomas wanted to knock them off, but had to trust the doctor knew what he was doing.

"Foolish mortal," Rees grumbled, appearing near Hugh's head. He patted the earl's hair back from his face. "Hurt Lord Bellemare with his potions."

"They are necessary," Thomas said. "He is the best physician I could find."

The bed linens were discolored with Hugh's blood and the earl's pale, unmoving body was a terrible sight in contrast to the stains. His neck and arm were bandaged with cut linen. Thomas regretted hitting him with his sword, but didn't know how else to get Lord Eadward off. His arm had caught fire when he'd swung and someone had doused him with water to put it out as his blade made contact. It had thrown Thomas' aim off just enough to strike his brother.

Needing something to do, Thomas went to Hugh's trunk at the end of his bed and opened it, hoping to find an extra bed linen to replace the bloodied one. Lifting a couple of Hugh's tunics, he felt along the edge, down toward the bottom.

"Can I be of service?" Rees appeared suddenly inside the trunk, sitting on a pair of Hugh's breeches. Digging around, he pulled out a vial of bright blue liquid. "Huh, I wonder why he never used this. I put it right in here nice and safe."

Thomas frowned, taking the vial. It was small, clear and cool to the touch. He lifted it to the light. "What is it?"

"A message," Rees said, as if the answer were quite obvious.

"Like a warning?" Thomas' frown deepened. "A warning from whom?"

"Nay, like a message," Rees said. "From the immortal realm. Halton and Gorman, your sister's sprights, delivered it."

Magic.

Thomas took a deep breath and stood, moving closer to the fire as he looked inside it. Tiny bubbles floated within. He shook it, still seeing nothing. "I cannot..."

"Well, you wouldn't like that, would you? Shaking it up and down." Rees snorted.

"How do you read it?"

"Read? You do not read message vials, you listen."

Thomas held it up to his ear.

"Not like that," Rees said, jumping up to grab it from Thomas. "It is a wonder you mortals communicate at all. Here, listen like this!"

"Wait," Thomas protested as Rees lifted his arm and tossed the vial on the stone floor. The container shattered and blue liquid spread over the stone, forming a small puddle. Smoke rose from the bubbling center, swirling until it formed the image of his pregnant sister.

"Juliana?" Thomas automatically reached for her. She looked pale and worried, her face slightly swollen from her condition, yet ever beautiful. His hand fell through her like air.

"Greetings, my brothers," Juliana said. Her voice was like a soft lullaby, a whisper from the past. Thomas stood in front of her, studying her face. Despite the pallor, she was attractive with long dark hair and wide blue eyes. Her eyes were like looking into his own. There was no doubt of their relation, though Juliana was definitely more feminine in appearance and demeanor than her brothers. The image of her stared straight ahead, not seeing him as she looked through him. "I hope this works. With the war, it has been hard to magically get messages out of our castle without them being seen and I would not have the Blessed King Ean thinking you were helping us. I love Bellemare and know you can understand my hesitance in seeing its blessing taken away. Unfortunately, my other alternative in communication was... Hmm, let us say that goblins are not the most trustworthy of couriers."

"Oh, aye," Rees nodded in agreement with her. "What she means is that they have been known to eat the messages. Trust me when I tell you that is one missive you do not want delivered."

Thomas grimaced, glancing down at the spright before turning back to his sister.

Juliana continued, "I discovered only this morning that my last two missives did not reach you. It seems the creatures I entrusted got hungry instead and it never arrived."

"Ah, see," Rees interrupted.

Thomas lifted his hand absently in the spright's direction, trying to get him to be quiet. He didn't want to miss anything his sister had to say.

"That is why I'm trying magic and intrusting this vial into the care of my sprights, Halton and Gorman." Juliana smiled and her attention was drawn to the side. She motioned her hand for silence, just as Thomas had done, and he assumed her own sprights were trying to interrupt.

Thomas again tried to touch her face, only feeling air. She turned her attention forward once more and he stayed in front of her, as if she truly looked at him.

"I had hoped for a happier message, but I send this to warn you, my dear brothers. Something is happening here in the immortal realm. King Lucien of the Damned is somehow gaining power. I do not have proof of the how, but Merrick feels it is so and I trust him in this. I have good reason to believe that the Damned King is planning to send demons into Bellemare."

Thomas swallowed. Her warning had come too late.

"I pray that you do not come upon them, but if you should, those that come in human form can most often be stopped by severing the head from the body or by fire." Juliana paused, looking down to touch her stomach, rubbing it in circles. "William I am sure you know how to put protective charms around the castle. Please do so if you have not already. You might need them."

"Juliana, what is it?" Thomas demanded, reading something dire in her expression. He reached to cover the hand on her stomach. As if sensing him, she stopped rubbing. "What is wrong, Juliana?"

"She cannot hear you, Sir Thomas," Rees said. "It is just a record of the past, not a link to the present Lady Juliana."

"Thomas," she continued, "I hope every day that you have recovered from your wounds. But you were always strong. There is so much I want to tell you, to try and explain. I do not want you to worry about me. Merrick is a good man. I know what you think of him being as he is the King of the Unblessed, but he cares for me and I for him. He saved your life, Thomas, that day on the battlefield." Juliana paused. Thomas already knew as much. "I am eternally grateful to him for that."

"Juliana." Thomas willed her to see him, really see him. She didn't. It was like Rees said, merely a record of the past. He wanted to hold her close, reassure himself that at least one sibling was safe.

"And Hugh," she sighed. "I hope that you have forgiven me for staying. Know that I made my choice and am happy in it. Whatever happens to me, this is what I wanted. You did not fail in your duty to me."

The image dissolved. Thomas tensed, lifting his hands as if he could stop it. "Nay, wait."

"That is it, Sir Thomas," Rees said.

"Something is wrong," Thomas said. "She is frightened. I could see it in her eyes. Juliana never talks like that. Something must have happened. Make it show me again. Bring her back."

"It only works once, Sir Thomas," Rees said. "Then gone forever."

Thomas sank to the floor, running his fingers through his hair. Not Juliana. He couldn't lose her, too. What was happening to his family?

A small flash appeared and Thomas automatically looked at the broken vial to see if there was more of the message. There was nothing.

"Lord Bellemare, I hate to see you like this." The soft, feminine voice drifted over him.

At the unexpected sound, Thomas shot to his feet, turning

toward the bed in the same motion. The mysterious woman with violet eyes was sitting next to his brother. She gasped, looking shocked to see Thomas in the chamber.

"What are you...?" Thomas began, ready to charge her and pull her away from his brother. She had a leech pinched between her fingers and a rivulet of blood trailed down Hugh's chest from where she'd pulled it off him. "What are you doing? Leave him be. The physician—"

The words never finished. The woman grabbed hold of Hugh and pulled his arm against her chest. Her lips moved, but no sound came out. It was as if she said, "I am sorry."

"Nay!" Thomas lunged on the bed, but he landed on the empty, blood stained coverlets. "Who are you? Why do you do this?"

She didn't answer.

"Rees!" Thomas yelled.

"Aye?" the little spright said.

"Why didn't you stop her?" he demanded.

Rees' big eyes teared. "I cannot. I'm just a spright. I'm sorry. I cannot. I do not have her power."

Realizing that yelling at the spright wasn't going to help his cause, he said, "I do not care how risky the journey is, find me away into the immortal realm. Now."

*Fire Palace of the Damned*

Hugh's body burned from heat and shivered from cold at the same time. It was an odd, contrasting sensation, but the only way his hazy mind could think to interpret it. Soft hands touched his face, but he couldn't see a person to go with them. Beneath him, his bed was hard, flat stone.

With each gentle caress the sharp pain that had wrapped him in darkness began to lessen. His neck no longer hurt and the soreness in his arm subsided. Though, deep inside, an ache remained—an ache in his soul, an emptiness he couldn't explain.

"I did what you asked," a woman's voice said. It sounded vaguely familiar. "He is alive, but barely. The men of his world know nothing of healing. They have sapped him of his strength."

"Leave us," a deeper male voice answered. "I will take care of the rest. Queen Tania will get what she asked for, but only too late will she know at what price."

"What are you going to do?" the woman asked. "Why have me save him, only to kill him?"

Why could not he see? Hugh tried to move, tried to open his eyes, but he couldn't. Still, he felt better as the bodily pain subsided even more.

"Do you not know me by now, Mia?" The man gave a cryptic laugh. "I am going to have my fun. Now, I suggest you leave me to it. I do not think this is anything you want to watch."

"Lucien, nay!" the woman answered. "You do not have to do this."

Hugh's mind was at instant attention. Lucien? The Lucien? King of the Damned? How did that evil being get into Bellemare?

Then, remembering that King Lucien couldn't go into the human world, Hugh was racked with fear. He was no longer at Bellemare. He was in the realm of immortals once again.

*Nay!* He tried to cry out. Lucien's sinister laugh answered the thought. It was as if he could hear inside Hugh's head.

"Lucien," Mia begged. "Please, I just healed him. Why—?"

A sudden, sharp agony hit Hugh's chest. He wanted to cry out at what felt to be the cut of a blade across his chest, but he couldn't. Mia screamed, her voice growing fainter as footfalls ran off into the distance. The woman had left him alone with the demonic king. He wasn't sure how he knew with certainty that they were alone, he just did.

"In my home at last, Lord Bellemare," Lucien said. "How I have watched and waited for you. Open your eyes to me. Look at me."

Hugh did, blinking in the dimmed firelight as he found the Damned King kneeling on the floor beside him. The hall was large and dark, unlike any human structure he'd ever seen in all his travels as a knight. The king's dark face was covered in ash and dust and the black pits of his demonic eyes burned with an inner fire. There was no mistaking his manlike features for those of a mortal. Only a devil could have eyes that burned in such a terrifying way.

"I have waited a long time to have you once again in my grasp, Lord Bellemare. But I confess, this is not how I imagined our meeting again." Lucien smiled.

Hugh moaned, trying to tell the king just what he thought of him. Lucien laughed. All around them was dark stone lit with a fire he couldn't see from his place on the floor. The low crackle filled the silence like the pits of hell threatening to consume at any moment. Lucien sat down on the floor next to him, leaning over on one arm to lightly swing a knife back and forth in his hands.

"How the blessed do fall," the king mused. "I look at you, in your fragile mortal body, so near death, so drained of life. What if I were to offer you eternity? What if I were to tell you that you did not have to face death or pain? That I could give you the power to take what you want, to have pleasure and flesh, to drink and kill without consequence? To keep your precious Bellemare intact and safe? And all you would have to do is ask me to give it to you in exchange for your soul."

Hugh grunted, though in truth there was a moment in which he wasn't sure what he would say. But, there was no way he could consider an offer from the devil. What good were all the things Lucien offered him without his soul? What pleasure was flesh without the willingness of it to be taken? What good was Bellemare without the moral code they lived by? What honor was there in killing without consequence or thought? And what good was living without the one thing every mortal craved—to love and be loved? He was an earl. He had the love of the people, the love of family, of the land of his generations past. No devil's offer could give him that. No devil's pleasures could honor what he had, what had been bestowed upon him by his ancestors.

The only thing he didn't have was the love of a woman, a wife, but he had the dream of it and hope was enough to make him wait for her. Until then, he had other pleasures—lust, laughter, companionship. Hugh thought of Tania. It was her fault that he hadn't taken companionship lately. She'd tainted him toward others. But, he knew that her memory would fade given time and another would catch his notice.

Tania wasn't a lady he could set above his hall at Bellemare. She had her own hall and her own land. He knew that from the beginning, from the first meeting when he'd looked at her and wanted her and she'd slapped him for daring to. Nay, never Tania for a wife. What reason was there to wish for more when it could not be? He would never consider the faery queen. He would marry a mortal, a noblewoman who loved like he wanted to love and who would honor as he honored. Like his father before him, he'd find a worthy lady to watch over Bellemare by his side, protecting the lands and the people as his ancestors had. Tania was an image of lust, a beautiful dream that would fade in the morning hours as reality took root. He was sure that when he married, his love would be born of the duty and honor of Bellemare.

Nay, the things he wanted could not be bargained for with King Lucien. The secret longing, which became vividly clear only now after Lucien threatened to take it all away, burned bright within him. He knew what he wanted, what he longed for. And it was nothing that could be found here in the realm of immortals.

"You disappoint me," Lucien said. "What I offer is better than the love you think of. What good is love when your lady wife dies? What good is love when Bellemare's blessing is stripped away and you are left with barren livestock and putrid soil?"

The jeweled hilt of Lucien's knife caught Hugh's attention. It was the dagger they'd given Juliana on her fourteenth birthday.

Juliana!

"Your sister and her husband are not here to save you." Lucien followed Hugh's eyes toward the blade in his hand. "Ah, you noticed that, did you? It is one of my favorite pieces. Your sister did use it after all to stop me last we all met in King Merrick's hall. What can I say? I am sentimental."

Hugh tried to speak.

"Oh, do forgive me," Lucien waved his hand over Hugh's throat. "You were saying?"

"How did you get that? Juliana had it last I saw her."

"That she did and so she did last I saw her as well."

"What have you done?" Hugh struggled for just an ounce of freedom in his limbs. It never came.

The fire burned hotter in Lucien's eyes for a brief second. "It is a surprise. You would not want me to ruin it, would you?"

Hugh cried out in pain and frustration. It had been so long since they heard from Juliana. Lucien screamed, a mocking sound as he joined the earl's rant of frustration. Hugh stopped and so did the Damned King.

"How disappointed I was when King Merrick chose her," Lucien admitted. "I had such hope for him, but I will confess I still do."

"I am not your priest. I have no wish to hear your confessions." Hugh looked away.

"Oh, but I think you will want to hear this," Lucien said. "I can feel how you dislike Merrick. You do not think he'll make your sister happy for long."

Hugh glared at him, resenting him because he was right.

"You are right to be frightened for Queen Juliana. A woman will only live so long in happiness with Merrick. He is the king of all that is unblessed and necessary evil is still evil. One day, she will wake up and realize what it is she married. And that is only if he doesn't grow bored of her first. Already it is rumored they do not share the same bed. Perhaps he is already done with her."

"I will take care of my family. They are no concern to you. If Juliana is unhappy, that is a family concern."

"Oh!" Lucien clapped, grinning and laughing in sinister glee. "That is what I love about you, Lord Bellemare. You are always the valiant knight. I cannot tell you how many temptations I put before you over the years—women, riches, power. All those chances and each time you rejected my demons' offers. I am honestly not surprised you rejected my offer to give you every whim in exchange for your soul. I would not want your soul if it was so easily seduced."

Hugh frowned. What was the king talking about? He'd never had dealings with a demon, well not since Nicholas.

"Ah, but you have," Lucien said. "In battle. Remember that time you rode up upon the women in the river? Naked, wet, helpless, beautiful women. You could have taken all three of them. I know you desired to do so. I made them enticing that way." Lucien waved his hand and suddenly the sound of frightened female gasps filled his ears. He turned his head away from Lucien only to see the hazy memory from his youth. Three naked women were in the water, just as he remembered them being—one blonde, one brown and one as fiery red as he'd ever seen. Lucien leaned close to his ear as he watched the silent memory. "You could have taken them and no one would ever know. You could have told yourself you were drunk on wine as you raped each of them in turn. But what did you do?" Lucien growled. Hugh watched as his younger self handed them a blanket and then pointed them on their way. "You let them go, no doubt saving the image to stroke your sword to later."

Hugh was about to answer when the three women turned to him. Their eyes lit with demonic fire and their faces turned to that of hags. His stomach tensed, realizing they'd been demons sent to lure him.

"You would have fallen that night and Bellemare's blessing would have ended." Lucien sighed. Hugh turned to see him frowning. "Every sin I threw at you, you resisted. No one has ever thwarted the attempts of my demons like you have, my lord. Like your family has. I knew then that yours were the souls strong enough to prove worthy of my full attention."

"Why are you telling me all this? Do you not know to never reveal your full intention to your enemy?"

"We will not always be enemies, my lord," Lucien said. "One day you will come to me and you will beg to join me."

"Never."

"Do not be so sure. There are ways to bend you to my will. I do not care if you know that I want you because when the time comes, you will offer yourself to me all the same. But for you, I make it easy. I tell you in advance that you will be honored amongst demons. Your fall from grace will be most great and because of it you will lead armies. I want you to rule with me, Hugh. I want you to rule your mortal world as I rule this one, answering only to me. Nothing that you do will be a crime, for you will make the law. You will control the demon armies. You will make the world cower in fear and awe. The whole mortal realm will worship you at Bellemare, the center of power."

Hugh tightened his jaw and stared at the dark beams of the ceiling. "Nay."

Lucien's pleasure faded and his eyes narrowed in annoyance. Hugh could tell the man didn't like to be naysayed.

"Or," Lucien continued, "you can beg me to take your soul in exchange for a favor and rule nothing. Either way, I get what I want. I always get what I want."

"Do your worst. I have no fear of death or pain."

"My worst will not be to you." The king's voice was a whisper, but the meaning was unmistakable.

Hugh looked at Juliana's blade. Did Lucien have his sister? Is that why she never contacted him? If Merrick let Lucien have her, he'd find the Unblessed King and kill him.

"Ah, see, this is the spirit that first baffled me. That goodness in you. The selflessness. I threaten you, tempt you and you do not budge, but one thought of those you love being in the slightest pain and you weaken." Lucien motioned to where the demon women's memory had been. Hugh turned his head, only to see a different memory—one where his horse was slaughtered in a skirmish. He'd been a little older by then and the stallion had been his favorite horse. Hugh saw his past self get up from the ground, fighting the man who had done it. He'd cut the man's face, surely deep enough to scar him if the blood were any indication. Then, his opponent fell, his sword tumbling away down a small ravine. His opponent's side surrendered, their horn sounding over the battlefield. "This is when I first realized that about you, first discovered your weakness. I came so close. You could have killed him and no one would have stopped you. He killed your horse. Why did you let him go?"

"You would never understand," Hugh said.

"Mayhap you are right," Lucien agreed. "Tell me anyway."

"Honor. His side surrendered. He was unarmed. The battle was over," Hugh said simply, though he was no saint. Even now, he still felt the desire to kill the man for the careless slaughter of his mount.

"He killed your favorite horse. That was the first horse you bred on your own. You took pride in that animal. I watched you with it. You loved that horse, trained it endlessly."

"And in the end the horse was only an animal, was it not? And that was a man." Hugh let his head roll so he again looked at the ceiling. Glancing at Lucien, he saw the Damned King studying the scene from Hugh's past. Confusion marred the king's face, as if he were really trying to understand. Was there something more to Lucien's obsession with the Bellemare family? Or was it simply just that—an obsession? "The church says animals have no souls and men do. It is what separates us from beasts."

Lucien shook himself, as if coming from a trance. The cold fire again returned to his eyes. Laughing, he said, "Far be it from me to contradict the mortal's church, but that was hardly just a man. But you did not know that, did you?"

Hugh turned to see the man who killed his horse looking at him. The knight's eyes lit with fire just as the three temptresses' had. He'd been a demon as well.

"There were others, many others, and each time you resisted." Lucien looked to be in repose, as if they discussed the passing of the moon. "So I knew I had to strike in another way. Little did I know fate would step in. Sweet Lady Juliana. How obliging of her to tempt King Merrick for me. And Nicholas, how he did grovel to the very thought of her! Pathetic little mongrel. You were right in not choosing him for her."

Hugh didn't like knowing King Lucien was so intimately familiar with his family's past. How did he know all this? How did he infiltrate their lives so completely? And more importantly, what vanity caused him to speak so openly about it now?

"Well, the hour grows late." Lucien sat up straighter. He took the knife. "Try to remember. After I release you, should you decide to join me, all you have to do is seek me out."

"Release me?" Hugh asked in surprise. He didn't expect that.

"Aye, but first..." Lucien lifted Juliana's blade and stabbed Hugh in the stomach. Hugh grunted, looking down. He couldn't feel the injury. He could scarcely feel anything. Lucien retracted the blade, leaving a wound that did not bleed. It was as if Hugh's body was frozen in time.

"Do not worry, that and the pain of your injuries will come back soon enough. I cannot deliver you into the hands of your captor unharmed." Lucien stood.

"My captor?" Hugh was beyond confused.

"Queen Tania." Lucien grinned. "She put a price on your

head and I will happily collect it."

Tania? Tania was the reason he was here? She ordered his capture? Rage poured out of him. Whatever tender thoughts he had of her fled with the knowledge of what she was doing to him. It wasn't enough that she'd detained him and he'd lost Juliana? Now, she had to do it again? Only this time, what would the cost be? William, Thomas and Juliana? He didn't have time for Tania's games, her mad plotting.

Lucien lifted his hands to the side. Smoke poured out of him as if his body smoldered. The king disappeared and the smoke rolled over Hugh's prone body. In his head, he heard Lucien say, "The sweet little faery made me an offer I could not refuse."

# Chapter Four

"Lord Bellemare, as promised."

Tania looked up from her throne. She'd sensed the Damned King coming, but she had not expected him to bring Hugh so soon. Instantly, she looked down at her gown to see if she was prettily dressed. Miniature sparks of light erupted from her wings, showering over her body. Faery pheromones were a natural reaction to desire. Detecting the dark lines that marred her skin, she was reminded of all that had happened and the momentary spark of pleasure faded. Lucien chuckled, catching her in the vain act. Steeling herself, she looked up.

"I see your interest in the earl is not just political," he teased. "You will send for me should he not live up to your expectations, will you not?"

Tania glanced down, seeing the hard press of sexual interest against the Damned King's tight breeches. Lucien waved his hand to the side. Dark energy flowed over the tarnished floor, pouring like smoke as an orange glow lit over the ground. Hugh appeared, his body unmoving as he lay on the great hall floor. Tania froze.

"The deal was that he would be alive." She stepped down.

"And he is," Lucien answered, only to shrug before adding, "albeit barely. You best hurry, pretty faery. He does not have long once I take my hold off him."

Tania crossed over to Hugh. "What has been done to him?"

"Walking dead," Lucien shrugged. "He was attacked at Bellemare."

"But, that means..." Tania shook her head. "That is not what I wanted."

"You said you wanted him brought to you alive. He is alive and delivered, as agreed. I have upheld my end of the blood oath."

"Not all of it." She realized too late that she should have specified Hugh, not just his family. "You cannot hurt his family."

"They have a fortnight," Lucien said. "When that fortnight is over, I am free to do as I wish and I will call upon you to uphold your part of the oath."

Tania glared at Lucien as she pointed down at the unmoving earl. "He will never forgive this."

"I know." Lucien waved his hand over his head, the sound of his dark laughter echoing over the tarnished hall as he disappeared. "You should be more careful what you wish for when making deals with the devil, my pretty faery queen."

Tania fell to her knees, shaking her head. Lucien was gone. She never imagined that the Damned King would go this far. But, she was foolish to have believed otherwise. Of course Lucien would do something like this.

"Lorelle, Jack, Robin!" Tania yelled, summonsing her faery subjects. Little bursts of light erupted all around her. "Help me, please. He is dying."

Tania held out her hands, trying to put her magic onto him, but her powers were weak. She focused her energy, but as it touched the earl's cool flesh, he thrashed and moaned. The queen jerked back, seeing that she'd turned his skin gray where she tried to heal him. Looking at her hands, and then to her surprised subjects, she pulled away.

"Heal him," she ordered. "Please, now. Do not let him slip."

The faeries ran their hands over the earl. Tania crawled away to sit on the steps leading up to her throne, unable to help them no matter how much she wanted to. She should've seen Lucien's tricks long before she made her pact. It had been too easy, getting him to hand over Hugh.

"Get the others!" She balled her useless hands into fists. "Robin, call the others. There needs to be more of you. Can you not see he is not going to make it? Please, I cannot lose him. I need him alive."

*I need him alive.*

*Black Palace of the Unblessed, Kingdom of Valdis*

Thomas' body jerked as he fell upon hard, black stone. The taste of the bitter potion was still in his mouth. Heinic swore it would take him to the immortal realm, delivering him right onto the Golden Palace of Tegwen's doorstep so he could speak with the Blessed King. As Thomas looked up, he knew the garden gnome had been half right. He was in the Otherworld, but not before Tegwen.

Thomas had landed alone, with only his sword for protection, on a long stone bridge that led to the front gate of the Black Palace. He could hardly be mad over his location. This was Juliana's home now. He'd have picked it if not for the gnome claiming he didn't remember the right mixture to get him there.

"Apparently, Heinic forgot the mixture to get me to King

Ean's palace," Thomas muttered, "not Merrick's."

The last time he'd been at the Unblessed King's castle he hadn't been outside, but he knew in his gut where he was. Thomas recognized the style of the twisted spires and the cut of the stone bricks along the wall. He'd been unconscious when he arrived at the castle the last time, having been injured in battle and saved by King Merrick.

Unlike Hugh, Thomas didn't hold any animosity toward Merrick, but he did fear him. As the king of necessary evil—the balance that kept both realms in existence—the Unblessed King still ruled evil. Such a kingdom had to mar a man's soul, even that of a dark elfin king.

Thomas glanced up. Long, twisted spires curled like gnarled fingertips toward the sky, hooked with spurs. Such creations were not possible to build in the mortal world. The sky was dark, but from what he understood it was always dark in Valdis. A full moon shone over the earth, lighting his way with the pale blue glow. The impression of mountains rose up over the distance, as if growing out of the surrounding forest. His legs shaking from the strange, dizzying potion travel, Thomas pushed himself up and walked toward the front gate.

Pointed lancet windows gave off a soft orange glow from within. In the center, above where a front gate should've been, was a large round window, carved in great detail to depict the silhouetted head of a dragon. There was no guard along the wall, no visible way to get inside.

Suddenly, the stone cracked and a giant wooden door formed, slowly creaking open. Thomas walked toward the narrow opening, peeking into Merrick's home. Within, the black stone seemed to swallow the torchlight into its depths. Thomas turned to the side, slipping into the castle through the narrow entry. The door slammed shut and when he turned, it was only stone, as if no entry had been there. Looking up, he saw the round dragon window was still where it should be. He found it odd that outside the orange glow had shone out, but now the blue moonlight shone in.

The narrow hall was bare, except for the decorative arches overhead. Thomas went with his gut, slowly walking down the hall. There was something to the air that made him think of Merrick, as if the man was in every stone, his magic thumping in the walls.

Hearing a cackle, he stiffened, pausing briefly before continuing on. The laugh sounded again. Thomas turned to face the noise, only to find the hall empty.

"Juliana?" he asked softly. "Juliana, it is Thomas."

"Sir Thomas!"

Thomas looked around. It wasn't his sister's voice that called out to him.

"Eh, down here!" a second voice said.

Thomas looked down. Two tiny sprights were on the ground, their voices nearly ten times as big as they were. Aside from their stature and a slight point to their ears, they looked like two small human males in bright green tunics.

"Remember us?" One of them pointed at his chest.

"Halton. Gorman." Thomas instantly remembered Juliana's two sprights. They talked constantly about everything but nothing relevant. Though annoying, they'd know where Juliana was.

"I told you he'd remember me," Halton said, his big blue eyes blinking rapidly.

"Nay, I told you, he'd remember me," Gorman protested.

"But he said my name first," Halton argued. "So he remembered me first and you second."

"Did not, Halton!"

"Did to, Gorman!"

"Did not!"

"Did to!"

"Ho!" Thomas interrupted the argument. "I need to find my sister. Can you take me to Juliana?"

"Juliana?" Halton slowly backed away, looking very guilty.

"Your sister, Juliana?" Gorman matched his friend's expression.

"Queen Juliana, you say?" Halton gave a small, guilty laugh.

The cackling noise he'd first heard sounded. Thomas turned, his hand on the hilt of his sword. Uneasiness washed over him. The sprights kept talking and he tried to listen past them, but it was hard.

"Oh, do not mind the goblins. They like scaring visitors," Gorman said.

"They like scaring everyone." Halton nodded in agreement.

"They do kind of scare me," Gorman gave a weak laugh, "but just a little and only if they scare you."

"Me? Nay, I am not scared of goblins."

"Aye, me neither."

"Where is my sister?" Thomas interrupted, having heard enough of their bickering. There was no time for this nonsense.

"Oh, well." Halton puffed out his chest at the tone. "This way."

"Do you hear the manners on that one?" Gorman whispered, though he was hardly quiet about it. "Methought he was the nice one."

"Nay, that was the earl. The earl was the funny one."

The two sprights led the way down the hall. Thomas kept an eye out for goblins. As they neared a doorway, the cryptic sound of laughter filtered over them. He was led into a great hall, Merrick's hall. Now this place he recognized, only it was fuller than he remembered. Small, withered looking creatures fell over themselves in merriment, the source of the sound.

"Ack, goblins," Halton grumbled, waving his hand at a low table full of the shrunken creatures. The tables were filled with bowls of live bugs and rotted vegetables. Thomas got a whiff of the stink and wrinkled his nose. At the end was a giant goblin, one much bigger than the others. A smaller, wrinkled goblin sat on the big one's shoulder.

Five giant fireplaces burned along the walls and giant Corinthian columns stretched up to the ribbed vaults of the ceilings, blocking the front of the hall from view. Thomas stepped forward, seeing an empty throne near the front. Keeping his eye on the creatures to make sure no threat arose, he grimaced to watch one suck a small, wiggling snake between his lips and swallow.

"Sir Thomas."

Thomas' head whipped around to the throne to see King Merrick now lounged where before it had been empty. Dark red tapestries had appeared behind him and he held a silver chalice in his hand, lifting it to sip from the cup.

"King Merrick," Thomas bowed in respect. "I was not expecting you to be home."

"Oh?" Merrick arched a brow. Suspicion lined his gaze. An upturned collar framed his face, reaching back behind his head, and leather bound back the locks of the king's unfashionably long blond hair, winding down the length from his temples to just above his waist. There were purple streaks in the blond, matching the embroidery on his black overtunic. "And where did you expect me to be if not at home?"

"With the war..." Thomas cleared his throat, not wanting to get into it. "I have come to speak with my sister."

"Juliana is busy now," Merrick said. The king's dark gaze pierced, hard and unforgiving. He was tan and, except for his clothing, he looked human. Thomas tried to see what Juliana did in the Unblessed King but it was difficult. The king was a very powerful man, but surely it just wasn't his power that drew Juliana. There had to be more. "We were not expecting you. As to the war, it is everywhere, as am I."

"Magic." Thomas nodded. It was hardly comforting knowing the king could be several places at once. Or was Merrick just claiming as much. It was hard to know what was true and what wasn't when it came to him.

"How have you been, Sir Thomas?" Standing, Merrick dropped the chalice. It disappeared before hitting the floor. His tunic was overly long, reaching to his feet. It was split open along the front to show black breeches and boots. The undershirt was royal purple, showing through the cross laces holding the tunic together over his chest. "You look better than when you left."

"Thank you," he answered.

"No effects?"

"Pardon me? Effects? You mean from the injury?" Thomas shook his head. "Nay, none that I know of. But, I never did get a chance to thank you for saving my life."

"You do not remember what happened, do you?" Merrick asked, tilting his head in question.

"Aye, I do." Thomas nodded. "I was injured in battle. You brought me here and I recovered. You saved me."

"Hmm," Merrick mused thoughtfully.

"That is what happened, it is not? Is there something I should know?" Thomas wondered about the look Merrick tried to hide.

"More or less, that is what happened," the king said. "And I did not do it for you. I did it for your sister." Merrick glanced over to his goblins before adding, "Because with you alive, she causes me less aggravation."

Thomas glanced back to the table. The goblins ignored them.

"She will want to see me," Thomas insisted, walking toward the king. Dark laughter rang over the hall and he again glanced back to see the goblins now watching him. Halton and Gorman were gone. "It is about our brothers."

Merrick shook his head. "She is not here, but I will tell her you came to see her. She will contact you when she is able."

"I must see her." Thomas thought of the message vial. Something had been in his sister's eyes when she made it. Juliana never talked like that. What was Merrick hiding from him? "Where is she?"

"She is the queen, we are at war," Merrick said. "I have her somewhere safe."

"And her child?"

"Our child is with her."

"And where is that? Why will you not tell me?" Thomas wondered at the tone. Merrick didn't hint what the child was, neither girl nor boy. It would seem a new father would show more enthusiasm for his firstborn. "What are you keeping from me?"

"If you must know, she is in the garden, surrounded by a maze you will never get through, protected by thorns as sharp as a sword blade that will slice you to pieces if you were even to try." Merrick sighed, sounding bored. "And, before you ask, Juliana will not be coming out anytime soon nor will she be receiving guests or messages other than the ones I give her. I do assure you, she is very safe where she is."

Assurances from the king of all that was unblessed did not comfort him. Mayhap Hugh had been right about the king. Mayhap Merrick was not to be trusted. What did they really know about Juliana's husband? It was clear the man wasn't going to let him talk to her. Thomas wanted to see his sister. He wanted his family.

Another loud shout of laughter sounded from the goblins. One of them yelled as fire sped by Thomas from behind. It was a ball of flames, flying through the air. He jumped back, turning to see a flaming goblin running toward him. The creature veered, heading back to the table only to dive into a bowl of slime.

Merrick sighed heavily and lifted his hand. A large transparent wall suddenly appeared between them and the goblins, blocking the noise out completely. The creatures rolled on the floor in laughter as the charred goblin pulled himself off the tabletop.

"Perchance, I may be of assistance, Sir Thomas," Merrick said, drawing Thomas' attention back to him. "What has happened to your brothers?"

"A woman with violet eyes took Hugh. William is missing and we suspect the same woman took him. Lord Eadward walked amongst us at Bellemare, but he was not alive."

"Hugh and William are missing and yet you are here." Merrick's gaze narrowed, suspicious. "Safe."

Thomas was not sure he liked the way the king said the words. There was something musing and cryptic to them. He stepped closer to the throne, lowering his tone to plead, "Can you help me find my brothers? Do you have the power to see them? Can you cast a spell or use your magic to find them? Please."

"Mia," Merrick said.

"Mia?" Thomas shook his head, confused.

"King Lucien's slave. I believe he said her name was Mia. She is a nymph with violet eyes. Though, hers are not exclusive to that color, she is the most logical choice."

"Is her hair dark as well?"

"Aye."

Thomas felt as if the room was caving in on him. Lucien had William and Hugh? It was his worst fear. "What does Lucien want with us?"

"Your souls, I would imagine. That is what demons do. They feed on souls. The more pious the soul, the more powerful the meal. The blessed Lord Bellemare's soul would make a fine trade for a Damned King, as would William the Wizard's."

"You have to help me," Thomas insisted. "I must find my brothers."

"I cannot help. Not with this. Lucien and I are not..." Merrick gave a short laugh. "We are not speaking. He will not give your brothers to me, nor would he tell me if he had them."

"There must be something you can do. Juliana would not see our brothers harmed," Thomas charged. "If you lov—" Merrick's hard look cut him off and it felt as if a hand strangled his throat, keeping him from speaking the words. The king's dark gaze searched him, almost pleading with him for silence. The pressure let up and he took a deep breath before continuing. "Please, help me."

Merrick closed his eyed briefly. Thomas realized he'd hit a sore point with the Unblessed King. His sister. There appeared to be more between the two than could readily be seen in Merrick. Mayhap the man did truly love her as Juliana claimed, despite his denial of it. Thomas had never met anyone like the Unblessed King before. He was a hard man to read.

"King Ean can track them better than I," Merrick said at last. "I have no hold on Bellemare, nor the people within the walls. I do not think I can help you. My men are busy fighting Tegwen. I cannot fight King Lucien as well, especially not knowing where or if he keeps William and Hugh."

"What about my sister? You tracked her."

"She made a pact with me, thus the shift in her," Merrick said. "With the rest of you, I cannot find you as easily. Were you nothing special, merely humans, it would not be a problem, but you are protected by King Ean. It makes it harder, especially with the magical defenses up because of the war. It is the same for Ean. He cannot find my subjects."

"You would send me to your enemy?" Thomas asked.

"You asked for my help and I am telling you where you should go for assistance."

"Can you get me an audience with King Ean?"

"Nay, but I can give you a guide that will take you close to his encampment." Merrick held out his hand. A small packet appeared in it, like a pillow made of blood red linen. "And I can give you this."

"What is it?"

"A way to reach me. Sprinkle it on yourself and I will know where to find you. But, I should warn you, it never wears off. Should you use it, you will be mine as much as you are Ean's. You will be marked as such and those who can detect such markings will know it. Some will think you cursed. Others will believe you are loyal to me. The blessed may possibly not trust you. Ean might take away his blessing of you, though I doubt he would take it from all of Bellemare over such a mark. However, I cannot control what he does so it is possible."

"Why would you tell me as much? Why not just throw it on me?" Thomas reached out to take the pouch. Rubbing it, he felt the inside. It was like a packet of dirt.

"Because telling you is what your sister would want me to do." Merrick lifted his hand, swiping it to the side. The clear wall disappeared and they were assaulted with the sound of laughter. The goblins had Gorman and were dipping the protesting spright head first into a bowl of bugs. "Now, leave. Lord Kalen rides with his Berserks toward the castle. They will not greet a blessed ward of Ean's as easily as I have, Juliana's brother or not. I will not have my men doubting me. Go. The troll will show you the way."

"Troll?" Thomas didn't like the sound of that.

"Volos," Merrick ordered. The giant goblin stood, easily towering over Thomas' height.

"Ah, troll." Thomas swallowed nervously.

"Bevil, come, I have a task for you," Merrick said. The small, wrinkled goblin on Volos' shoulder looked up. The great beast plodded toward them, carrying the smaller creature. Thomas took an involuntary step back, moving out of the troll's direct path. He touched the hilt of his sword, drawing some comfort from the weapon, but not much. "Take him to the edge of Ean's encampment and leave him."

Bevil instantly gave Thomas a nasty little grin.

"Unharmed." Merrick sighed in exasperation. Bevil's grin fell into a pout. As if answering an unasked question, the king added, "And aye, that does mean you cannot have a taste of his flesh. I want him left intact and unharmed."

Volos grumbled and Bevil leaned over to whisper into the big troll's ear. The troll started to chuckle. Thomas' gut tightened in fear. Somehow, he didn't think he wanted these creatures happy.

"Before I go, promise me that Juliana is safe," Thomas beseeched Merrick. "Give me your word. Please."

"She is as safe as the Unblessed Queen can be at this exact moment." Merrick's words were hardly comforting. Thomas had the sense that the king hid something, but arguing with him wasn't going to get him anywhere. All he could hope was that King Ean would shed some light on matters. "Now go. Bevil will take you through the goblin's entrance so the Berserks won't see you leave."

"Tell my sister I love her," Thomas said before turning to follow the goblins out.

"I do not know if she will hear it," Merrick answered when Thomas could no longer hear him. He didn't know what to make of the visit and found it very strange that Thomas evaded capture by the Damned King, yet William and Hugh were in his grasp. Still, what else could he do but look into matters? If Lucien sent Thomas to trick him, he would fail. Merrick had turned out his own brother, his flesh and blood. Compared to that, nothing would stop him from turning his brother-by-marriage away.

Letting his flesh dissolve into a fine mist, he drifted out of his hall to a crack in the floor. It was a place only his magic could pass through. Going to the darkest depths of the castle, he solidified, standing near his dungeons. Only a few prisoners were kept locked behind his walls. They'd been held since before he'd become king and were too insane to release, so there they stayed for all eternity.

A small, portly goblin wobbled by. He looked up, his eyes completely white. Werdan was the prisoners' caretaker. Merrick ignored him as he walked down the hall. The curved ceilings were low and he ducked his head under the arched doorways. If he wanted, he could've made the ceilings taller by mere will, but he did not dare change a single brick. To do so would be to risk one of the prisoners slipping out of their cells.

At the end of the long hall, he came to a metal door. Lifting his hand, he started to knock, only to stop when it opened from within. An old, blind witch lived in this part of the palace—never leaving her room. The door creaked as the witch turned her face toward him knowingly. She had short white hair and a band of white material covered the empty sockets of her eyes.

"My king." The woman's voice was raw and grating. She sniffed in his direction. "You come for help?"

Merrick wasn't surprised that she knew he was there. In her blindness, she saw many things. Though she could not be trusted completely, she was very powerful and worth keeping around. "Aye."

"Oooh, aye, aye." The witch reached forward to touch his chest. Merrick resisted the urge to pull away. The woman smacked her lips, cackling as her bony fingers patted right above his heart. "How is our queen?"

Merrick didn't move.

The witch's laughter grew as she patted him harder. "Oooh, broken."

Merrick stepped back and her hand fell away. Her pleasure faded from her dry, wrinkled lips. "I am not here about Juliana."

"But—"

"I am here to see if you can locate someone for me." Merrick did not want the woman to utter another word about his queen. Every fiber in his being told him not to trust her with Juliana. "Can you help me or not?"

"Go away," the witch said. "You have nothing I can use."

"I'm sure you can think of something." Why was he even here?

"I get more from not helping with this—much amusement." She tried to shut her door. Merrick put his hand on the metal, holding it open. "If they die, you will have to tell her you did not help to find her brothers."

"I cannot find them," Merrick said.

"Do you think that will matter when she learns you did not even try?" The witch slammed the door. Merrick hit the metal hard several times, much to her amusement. Then, growling, he waved his hand, taking away the new gown he'd given her as payment for helping to save Thomas' life a year ago. It was replaced by the tattered, old garment she'd owned before. The witch screamed the instant it happened, her laughter dying.

"You enjoy my misery, witch," Merrick strode away from her, "and I shall enjoy yours."

Pleasure rippled over Lucien as he walked through the hall of his home. The faery queen had thought to use him, but he wasn't a fool. He was the master of deceit, the king of treachery. A mere faery couldn't best him, though he knew she'd still try.

The knowledge that Mia was chained in his bedchamber, trapped in the tight leather he liked to keep her in, made arousal flood through his veins, combining with the joy of his misdeeds. She'd hate him now because he'd made her atone for betraying him. The nymph's treachery in sneaking off to Bellemare to warn William angered him, but it also pleased him to know that her defiant spirit wasn't completely killed. He liked it when she fought him, but even more when she fought herself and her desires.

He thought of the faery queen, part of him wishing she would have taken him up on his offer. What pleasure it would have been to bring her low, teaching her the sin that would forever mar her and make her his ally. Her mind was close, on the edge of faery sanity. He could have forced her. The queen's magic was down after all. He could have bent her over the throne and forced the carnal knowledge of what he offered onto her. Greed kept him from acting. Deflowering the little faery wasn't necessarily the best use of her maidenhead, though it would have been entertaining.

Coming to the bedchamber door, he knew that Mia's sweet body would do to ease the ache in his loins. The taste of her fall was better than any frigid queen. He threw open the door, finding her right where he had put her. Chains held her thighs open as she lay on the bed on a sea of dark brown fur. Her hands were bound over her head. Thin leather straps crossed from her shoulders down between her thighs, barely covering her nipples and doing nothing to hide the thatch of hair guarding her sex.

Her wide violet gaze found him as he entered. Dark black kohl lined her eyes, making them almost glow. Lucien let his shirt disappear as he approached her. Gauze blew toward the bed, the material unharmed as it drifted over the suddenly bright fires.

"I see your temper is better, my king." Her expression was defiant as she faked boredom.

*Mmm, good, she is going to fight me.*

"I have other things that need sated, my sweet nymph," he assured her, "so that my temper may truly be eased."

Her gaze moved down to his erection. He let his pants melt

away so he stood naked before her. The arousal towered from between his thighs in desperate need of release. But there was another need, the need to conquer her yet again, to show her that he could have her, could control her and she couldn't resist no matter how hard she tried. Mia was his. She would always be his, until he sucked her soul completely and left her for dead, or until she succumbed to his will for her.

The memory of her lips on William the Wizard's fueled his need. She breathed hard, her back slightly arched. He allowed her chains to loosen their hold so she could move. Flames appeared in his palm, and he slithered them like a snake down his arm and over his naked chest to encircle his arousal. The heat felt good against his flesh.

"I have no wish to sate you, my king," Mia hissed.

Lucien took a deep breath, letting his eyes fill with black. "Your smell says otherwise."

"You are imagining things." She sat up, inching away from him. The chains on her legs didn't let her get far.

"Would you prefer to play with the demon?" he asked, crawling onto the bed. "It begs me to let it out, to let him have you. I should after your deceit."

She stiffened, not answering.

"Do not you want to hear what I did with the earl?"

"Did you..." She hesitated and he felt the caring in her, no matter how she tried to suppress it. He held on to that feeling, studying it. The emotion wasn't like what he carried inside him. Licking her lips, she took another route, arching a brow. "How is the earl's soul?"

"Intact."

That surprised her. Lucien watched her face and though her expression didn't change, he could feel that her insides did.

Was that relief she felt? The feeling angered him. Why should she feel relief over the earl's soul? Why should she care so deeply what happened to the people of Bellemare?

"I had better use for him. I delivered him to Tania. The faery is close to turning and I believe his rejection will be just the thing to plunge her into darkness. Faeries are such predictable creatures—so flighty, so driven by the pursuit of happiness and pleasure. Combine that with a virgin queen who must sacrifice her own pleasure for the sake of her race's magic until she has found her mate, and you have a volatile situation." Lucien let fire burn in his gaze as he watched Mia, feeding off her reaction to his words. Knowing he was stretching the truth, he said, "The faery queen seeks to trap him in this realm with her. If she succeeds, Bellemare will be without its earl. If she does not, the faery queen will fall into darkness and the veil that keeps me from the mortal world will lessen with her faery magic. It will only be a matter of time before I find my way through to Bellemare and the rest of the mortals. Regardless of what happens, the Bellemare souls will be mine."

In truth, Hugh would never go back. Lucien had made sure of that. But, if Mia warned the human like he thought she might, it would put a rift between the faery queen and Lord Bellemare.

Suddenly, Mia laughed, a sound dark enough to rival his own. "He would not beg you to take his soul no matter how much you tortured him, would he? Lucien, I am surprised...surprised you are losing your touch."

"Fear not, little nymph. It is all arranged. I am close to getting my Bellemare soul."

"Oh?" Mia arched a brow. "You think the earl will fall into your hands so easily? You gave him to the faery queen. She can block your magic."

"Who said I was talking about the earl?"

Her mocking smile faded. "What have you done?"

"You know the price of knowledge. Care to barter?" Leaning over, he licked her leather-covered nipple, pushing the strand aside with his tongue. Mia gasped. Against her flesh, he said, "Your choice, Mia. The demon or the man, but one way or another you will be sating this body tonight."

"The man," she answered without hesitation, her eyes closed.

He heard her, but he demanded anyway, "What was that, sweet little nymph?"

"The man," she said louder. "I would sate the man."

"Prove it." He let the sound of demons enter his voice, just as the chains disappeared from her body. Mia growled, slapping him hard. Lucien's head fell back in pleasure and arousal. He lifted his arms to the side. She hit him again and again, scratching him with her nails to draw blood. The wounds healed as fast as they were inflicted. Snarling, he grabbed her by the arms and threw her down.

"I hate you," she swore. "I will see you damned."

"Sweet Mia." He chuckled, his tone as dark as his soul. "I already am damned. There is no hell for me beyond this. If you truly wish to curse me, say you will see me blessed."

His mouth opened and he looked at her for a long moment before capturing her lips. The demon tried to surface, but he pushed it back. Tonight he would give her the man not the beast. Even as he thought it the power within him surged once more and he couldn't resist its addictive pull.

She bit his lip hard, drawing blood, and he shoved her legs open in response. The salty taste of him mingled in their kiss. Her body was wet, ready to take him any way he pleased.

"Tell me," he ordered.

"Why must I say it?" Her mouth chased his as he pulled up.

"Say it."

"I love you, Lucien, and I resent myself for it."

Lucien smiled, kissing her hard as he thrust within her. He took his pleasure in her body, knowing she would find hers. His sweet nymph could never resist him.

"Lux lexis," William mumbled, frowning. "Lix lucis."

He knew he was close, if he could only remember the right words. It was much harder to work magic without his wand and only a few spells would work. His body was sore from the chains holding him against the wall and it had been far too long since he'd eaten anything. He did manage to get some sleep, but it was hardly comfortable upright.

"Ah, I know!" He smiled, saying boldly, "Lux lucis."

A soft glow illuminated his whole body, throwing light over his prison. Expecting to see a dark and lonely tomb of a cell, he gasped in surprise. "Well, who do we have here?"

Next to him, a man was chained to the wall. He didn't move, but his color was too good for him to be dead. Seeing a pointed ear, but not much else as the man's long hair hid his face, William knew the man to be an elf. He leaned forward, seeing what looked like two more pairs of feet beyond his neighbor's. Since none of them had moved that William had heard, it was clear they were under some sort of enchantment.

"Just my luck," William grumbled as the soft light over his

body began to fade. “My only company is under a spell. Now, I don’t suppose any of you happen to remember the spell to make food appear?”

The thought was punctuated by the growling of his stomach, as the glow around him faded and he was cast into darkness once more.

# Chapter Five

Tania fluttered above the bed where Hugh rested. She had his body cleaned of the dried blood that had remained after his healing; watching carefully to make sure none of the faeries touched him too long in any one area. She hated feeling jealous, but she couldn't seem to help it. After sucking the health from him and turning his flesh gray when she tried to heal him, she was scared of touching his flesh in case she did more harm than good. After his bath, she had him moved to her bed, where he now rested.

Her bedchamber was at the top of the palace. Sometimes it was as high as the treetops, at others no taller than the crown of a mushroom. Though, personally faeries were one of their two sizes—either big or small. They couldn't make themselves into giants, unless within the castle and then all would grow the exact same amount as the stone walls, keeping them in proportion. The changing palace was what kept them hidden in the forest. They could all become a single grain of sand, completely unseen unless one knew where to look.

Tania continued to hover over the prone earl. The bed Hugh rested on was in the middle of her chambers. The floor shone like ice, though it wasn't cold. It matched the frosted crystal walls. Though smooth to the touch, the walls were uneven, like a clustering of icicles.

Along one side of the room was a bathing pool. It was normally surrounded by green vines but the walls of the silver palace were not all that had changed with her mood. Once bright with vases of flowers and lovely vines, the plants no longer blossomed. The pool was scented and the water never needed changing, as it magically renewed itself. Near the pool, lounging chairs and fluffy floor pillows stuffed with feathers were on a platform. She used to entertain her special guests there, away from the court below. On the other side of the bed was the door to her tall wardrobe where her many beautiful, now neglected, gowns hung. Sewn with the thread of silk spiders, the lovely white dresses shimmered with the twinkling of stars. Only faeries knew the secret of weaving such magnificent fabric.

When she dressed that morning, she barely noted the thin material of the gown she'd materialized from the wardrobe to come over her. Now, with Hugh there, she looked at herself. The bodice was light, decorated with tiny cloth flowers over her breasts. The skirt flowed freely around her waist and hips, reaching to her calves. Beneath the gown, she was naked, a fact that had never been as noticeable to her as in that moment.

A silk blanket covered Hugh's legs and waist, but she knew he was naked beneath. His color was better with the dark tan once more in his muscled flesh. Tania bit her lip, staring at his chest. The last time she'd seen him like this, he'd been shackled to a bed, held her prisoner when she'd helped Juliana escape. He looked every bit as handsome as he did then. His dark brown hair was longer and there were smudges under his eyes, but she didn't care.

Her stomach tightened, aching terribly. It remembered Lord Bellemare in ways her mind couldn't. He'd kissed her, thought the most deliciously wicked thoughts of her. She knew the first moment he stepped into her hall that she wanted him and that he wanted her. Their minds connected and she'd heard his thoughts—not all, but the ones he had about her. That had never happened to her without the casting of a spell.

Now, Tania's wings fluttered so fast she hovered above his prone form. Her body was slender and she was taller than the rest of the females of her kind, even some of the men. Still, when she was in her larger form and had both feet rooted on the ground, the top of her head only came to the earl's chin. His chest was so broad she would barely be able to wrap her arms around him.

Moisture gathered between her thighs, just as it did whenever she thought of him. But now it was worse because his naked flesh was so close. His smell engulfed her senses, drawing her down to be closer to him.

Over the last year, she'd looked her fill of him, secretly watching from the stone island in the middle of the divination pool as he undressed. It was wrong of her, she knew that, but she was fascinated with watching him pleasure himself, his hand fisting his arousal, his muscled body flexing as he lay on his back, as he braced his hand against a wall, as he bathed, even once in the forest. Such a sexually virile man would unquestionably make for a fine lover. Tania had touched herself as she watched him, but the relief she found was temporary compared to the desperate need to feel his flesh that came over her.

Little sparks of pheromone erupted from her wings, showering over him. She flew down, landing on the bed. Lowering herself so she was on her knees, she knelt beside him on the stuffed mattress. He didn't move.

Tania couldn't stop herself as she touched his chest. Waiting to see what would happen, she was pleased that her contact didn't hurt him like before. He was hot beneath her fingers, his flesh dark compared to hers. She touched a small nipple, watching it bud beneath her fingers. Then, curious, she glanced down to his waist.

Hugh would be asleep awhile longer. He'd been so sick and the healing had taken much out of him and her faeries. What harm was there in a closer inspection? It wasn't as if he'd know.

Tania lifted up off the bed and hovered over his body, drifting down so she was above his legs. Taking the silk covers, she pulled them to the side. His male pride lay soft between his thighs. The faery queen lightly caressed his hip, letting the tips of her fingers dance closer to his member as she gathered her courage. The shaft was softer than she imagined it would be as she took it in her hand.

Tania bit her lip, rubbing him gently before moving to feel his hard, flat stomach. Her hand flush against him, she explored his abdomen, noting little scars along his tight frame. The man was a fighter and his flesh bore the marks of such a life.

Hugh's heat beckoned her and before she realized what she was doing, she'd lowered her legs over his, her knees pressing tight alongside his thighs. The skirt of her gown was loose, allowing room for her to move freely. The material covered his stomach, concealing his shaft.

It was too much to finally have the earl within her grasp. The memory of his kisses was as strong as the day he'd given them to her. Wiggling, she angled her sex to lightly touch his, only to pull back in surprise to feel it was warmer than it had been in her hand. She looked down, lifting her skirt to discover that it had grown in length, hardening like it did when she watched him alone.

Tania hadn't meant to arouse him, not when he was recovering from Lucien's cruelty. But to see his reaction to her, the base desire, she quivered. Her wings fluttered wildly, showering them again in pheromone. Pushing her hands over the firm planes of his chest, she explored his jaw. It was rough beneath her fingers. A light moan of sheer sexual pleasure escaped her.

Just a kiss. One simple kiss and she would leave him to rest.

Tania leaned down, torn between her anger toward his rejection, the anticipation of his nearness and the fear that she couldn't make him love her. She looked at her hand, seeing the dark lines that had formed. The markings on her flesh had not lessened with his presence.

With her mouth inches from his, she stopped to listen to him breathe. She hesitated and did not move to close the distance. Stolen kisses when he was asleep were not what she brought him here for. She touched his still lips, running her fingers across the firm length. Pulling them away, she pressed her hand to her own lips.

"I waited for you." An ache filled her. Why did she still hurt? He was here, in her grasp. She shouldn't hurt anymore. The pain should have left her. A tear slipped over her cheek as she whispered down to him. "I waited and you never came back like you promised to do. What does Bellemare have that I do not? What pleasure does it offer you that I cannot give to you? What beauty does it hold that I cannot make for you? Am I not beautiful enough for you? Why do not you want me?"

The lines on her body grew, vining across her waist and hip. She could feel them burning as they moved. There was no need to see them to know they were there. Another tear slipped from her eye, falling across his cheek. Hugh jolted beneath her, groaning as he blinked to wakefulness.

Dark brown eyes met hers, filtering with confusion as he

looked at her face. Glancing down his body, then again at her, he frowned. Tania waited breathlessly to hear what he would say. It reminded her of the first time she'd detained him in her palace, when she'd had him beneath her just like he was now. Only this time he wasn't bound to the bed. His arms were free and she didn't have the magic in her to restrain him.

His mouth opened, as if he would speak. A low moan sounded as he grabbed her by the arms, jerking her forward to his mouth. Tania gasped at the sudden impact of his lips to hers. He kissed her hard, plundering her mouth with his tongue, biting her lips with his teeth. She barely had time to react before he was rolling her beneath him. Her wings crushed, bending awkwardly beneath her back, but she didn't care.

Hugh's naked body covered hers, pinning her down. His thighs pressed along the outside of hers, trapping her so his thick erection burned into her hip. If she wanted, she could shift into her smaller form and escape, but her mind was lost and she couldn't remember how to perform the simple little trick.

He let go of her arms, only to reach between them. She felt him tugging on her gown, lifting the skirt, as he maneuvered his thighs to settle between her legs. He broke the kiss, moving to lick at her jaw and neck. Tania's eyes opened wide, shocked by the sudden onslaught of pleasure and heat she felt. Never had she imagined a man's kisses would feel like this, so commanding and sure. The weight of his body pressed in on her, making her burn wherever their flesh met. She was scared, exhilarated, unsure.

Hugh pulled at the delicate bodice of her gown, ripping it to free a breast. With a deep groan, he wrapped it in his palm, rubbing the globe hard only to pinch the nipple between the side of his thumb and finger. He moved his kisses from her neck to her chest, tearing the bodice more as he freed the second breast. Warm lips covered her nipple, sucking and moaning against her flesh as if he would devour her whole. She wiggled beneath him, her legs held open by his strong thighs.

Touching his shoulders, she lightly caressed his arms. His hand slid from her breast, continuing to rip its way down over her waist until the entire front of her dress was torn and her body exposed. Hugh explored her hip, each touch passionate as he moved to wet her other nipple with his hot kisses.

The earl didn't speak, save for the animalistic grunts that sounded each time he moved. He pulled away, his eyes closed as he took her hand and forced it down between them. His breathing deepened, becoming harsh, as he put her hand to his erection. It was big in her palm and no longer soft. The earl resumed his kisses on her chest, rocking himself against her palm. She kept her eyes wide, overwhelmed with sensations. Pleasure hummed within her flesh until every piece of her seemed to be under his spell. Nothing had ever felt as good as the temptation she found in his arms.

Then, he reached down between her thighs and thrust a finger into her sex. The action bumped her arm aside and she let go of his arousal. She was wet for him, but the sudden penetration took her by surprise. Hugh groaned, louder than before as he circled his finger inside her tight body.

"Hugh." She suddenly panicked.

"Aye," he groaned, removing his finger. The way he said the word gave her the impression that he wasn't answering her so much as talking to himself.

Taking his shaft in hand, he guided his sex to hers. She tensed, not made to wait long before he was thrusting in. Hugh lifted up on his hands, angling his body better to hers. The intense length of his erection stretched her, making her burn deep inside where he touched. She wiggled beneath him, somewhat trying to get away from his impaling member. He gripped one of her hips, holding her still.

"It has been so long," he mumbled, over and over. "So long, so long..."

Working back and forth, he eased his way in, not gentle but not brutal either. Finally, he pushed deep, filling her as he seated himself to the hilt. A loud cry left him and he started pumping, as if mindless of what he was doing.

"Hugh?" She was torn between the pressure he caused and the pleasure she felt.

He bent his knees, holding her open as he leaned over and captured her mouth. Though passionate, he gentled his hold, slowing so her body could build to join his. Tension focused in her lower stomach, as he reached between them. His finger circled her clit. Tania tensed, her body convulsing in orgasm. Hugh groaned in approval, his mouth smiling against hers as he too began to jerk with release.

His lips hovered over hers as he breathed hard, not moving. She lightly touched his arms, reveling in the sensations of their joining. Hope blossomed inside her, sending energy out over her room. The vines and flowers drank of her power and perked up.

"You got what you wanted from me," Hugh said, not opening his eyes. He was still inside her, his body covering hers. "Now let me go."

*What?* Tania pulled back to study his face.

Hugh rolled off her, not looking at her as he sat on the bed. He put his head in his hands. "Where are my clothes?"

Tania watched him, not sure what she was waiting for him to do. She pushed up from the bed, feeling the ends of her tattered gown tickling her flesh as it fell aside. The clothes were unwearable.

"They were too bloody. I had them thrown out." She reached to touch him, only to stop as she saw her hand. The dark lines on her flesh hadn't faded. She drew her hand back to her lap, itching at it as she tried to rub the marks off. How could it be? They'd joined. The darkness within her should be gone. Her full power should've come back. The goodness and happiness should've come back. She looked at the vines. They had perked up, but they were still wilted and didn't bloom. Arching her back, she stretched her crushed wing, fluttering it back and forth to straighten it.

"Do you think nakedness will trap me in your palace?" Finally, he turned to look at her. There was no love in his eyes for her, only an emotionless resistance. Hugh paused and she saw his eyes following some of her lines. Why hadn't this worked? Why hadn't she changed? Why didn't he? "You will be better off trying to restrain me again, only this time I will know it is coming and I will not be as merciful when I find my freedom."

Her gaze narrowed in anger.

"You have nothing to say, queen?" Hugh stood from the bed, completely naked and seeming not to care. Derisively, he drawled, "Well that is wonderful, is it not?"

"What do you expect me to say? You are being hateful." She crossed her arms, pouting out her lip.

"Me? I am hateful? You are one to talk, Tania. You join forces with the King of the Damned, kill my horses, do something to my brother, haunt me like a spirit only to have me beaten and kidnapped, and then have the impudence to tell me I am being hateful? Aye, I do hate you and what you have done to me and my family. Every time you are near I lose someone I care about. First, you send Juliana to that monster. And now William is missing." His eyes were hard, his body rigid. "All I can determine is that you do all this because you are bored and wish to amuse yourself with me and my family. You are a wicked being, Tania. You stole my sister from me just to be part of some faery tale story between Juliana and Merrick—a man, by the way, who can never love her, and now you take my brother. What will you do with William? What have you done? Where did you send him? To the giant Lord Angus? What faery tale do you think to be part of now?"

"You liked me well enough to take me to bed," she charged. How could he have done that while hating her?

"Please tell me that is not why you brought me here. Tell me it wasn't to finish what you started between us a year ago."

"I started?" she gasped. "You—"

"Oh, by all that is holy, that is it, is it not? You brought me here for this." Hugh motioned toward the bed.

"You do not love me," she said, confused. How could he think she'd do all that to him? Aye, she sent Juliana to Merrick. She did want to be part of their love story. It all worked out. They were married. Juliana was a queen. As for love, Merrick was born of light, he could love, couldn't he? Or had she made a mistake with that one? She wasn't so sure anymore. Everything was confused inside her—her powers, her emotions—and it kept getting worse each time Hugh said he hated her. Did her deal with Lucien somehow cause these events he spoke of? She didn't mean for anyone to be hurt. She only wanted to see Hugh, to talk to him, to ask him why he never came back like he promised.

But, he spoke of William. She didn't take William. She knew that.

"Love you?" he spat. "I do not even like you, Tania. How could I? You threaten everything I have ever cared about. Bellemare and my family are the only things I have ever loved.

Now my family is broken up, my lands are threatened, the pride of our family—the horses—are dying. The dead walk..."

As his words tapered off, he shivered. She looked down at her lap, slowly pulling the sides of her gown to cover her body from view. Lucien had said the earl had been attacked by the walking dead. Was that her doing? Did her hunger to have him cause such an event? He claimed to love only two things—Bellemare and his family. Hadn't his actions in choosing the manor over her proven that? Her heart ached, a horrible feeling inside her chest, and still she did not want to accept what he was saying, even as she heard it from his own lips confirming what she knew to be true. The earl did not love her.

Hugh hated her.

He hated her.

"And there is no room in you for anything else, is there?" She tried to keep the emotion from her voice, but it was hard. *No room to love beyond those two things? Bellemare and your family.*

"Why would you even care?" Hugh asked. "You are nothing more than a bored, silly faery who takes sick pleasure in tormenting me. What do you know of my responsibilities? What do you care of my honor and duty?"

Tania shot up on the bed, lifting off as her wings beat hard in the air. She glared at him, wishing she had the magic to hurt him as he hurt her. But, even now, she couldn't strike out. This was all too much. His words killed the physical pleasure she felt, but her body was still renewed by sexual release and she used that energy now. Hugh held his ground, even as the lines of her sorrow crossed completely over her. Seeing her reflection in the glassy floor, she stiffened. Her eyes had gone completely black and her wings no longer held any white. They were gray with black threading to completely replace the silver. Her gown mended itself, stringing across her body to cover her even as it left gaps of flesh showing through the ripped holes along the front. The material grayed, no longer pretty and white, but dingy and dark.

Tilting her head, she looked at him. "That which has been taken cannot be given back. You will remain here, my lord. You can never go back to Bellemare."

Hugh didn't move as Tania poofed into a little ball of light and buzzed off like an insect. He was so angry at her, yet frightened of her at the same time. The woman was flighty, to be sure, but she also had powers—magic that he as a mortal man did not begin to understand the depths of.

*That which has been taken cannot be given back.*

So she did know where William was. Or did she refer to Juliana? Anger boiled within him at the knowledge of her pact with Lucien. What did this faery want with him? Why him? Because he'd wanted her so fiercely the first time they met, to the point he could think of little else for the last year?

Today, when he awoke with her temptress body hovering over his naked one, it was clear that she'd been seducing him while he slept. Even as he knew he shouldn't succumb, he couldn't resist her pull.

Though strange, the black lines on her body hadn't detracted from her beauty. She was still small and delicate, just as lovely as the first time he walked into her great hall and was hit with instant desire. Images had flashed through him of that first meeting, images of her pleasuring him before her throne, images of dominating her. They had been mere fantasies, but she'd slapped him for them. That's when he discovered she could read his thoughts—those particular thoughts anyway.

So, what? She decided she finally wanted to act on what

was between them? But why go to these lengths to get him into her bed? She'd been the one keeping him at arm's length. Or was this to punish him for daring to desire her at all? What was it she'd said that first day they met?

*Lord Bellemare should not have such thoughts without invitation to do so.*

Was all this because he didn't ask her permission to fantasize about her? It's not like these faeries were innocent little maidens who didn't know about the ways of men. Thomas and William both told stories about the carnal appetites of the faery race. He was sure that it was some of those stories that prompted his obsession with Tania to begin with. Already he'd been attracted to her and add to that desire a year full of thoughts of her being a carnal and insatiable being? It was like throwing tinder on the blazing fire of his lust.

Thinking of it made him want her again, which only served to anger him more. She acted as if he were some plaything. He was a man with responsibilities. There was no time for these games. He had Bellemare to run, his family to take care of. He needed to get back to both.

*You will remain here, my lord. You can never go back to Bellemare.*

Angrily, he screamed, hoping she heard him. She would not keep him prisoner here. He had to get back. How could he live without his family?

Looking to where Tania had left, he frowned. The last change in her was disturbing—the eyes filling to black where the white should be, the ashen skin tone. He'd seen the same changes on Lucien. William had said Tania was a neutral party, but it seemed his brother was wrong about this. She definitely had ties to the Damned King, ties they had not seen the year before. Had it always been there? Or was it a cause of the war that raged between the blessed and unblessed?

Feeling confused and helpless, he sat on the bed and buried his head in his hands. His body was weak and the memory of Lucien's visit was all too real. There were so many factors and yet he couldn't make sense of half of them. This wasn't his world. He didn't understand the immortal realm, or the magic it carried. He was a man, a mortal and he was out of his element. Hugh didn't like being out of control.

"We fight a war that has no goal other than to be fought because it must be." Merrick looked around the center clearing of his garden, avoiding the platform in the exact middle that used to hold a divining basin given to him by King Lucien.

Silver moonlight bathed the withered and neglected plants of the black gardens. Dark stone paths led up from his castle palace, twisting about the grounds in a seemingly endless pattern, surrounded by thick walls that formed a labyrinth from which trespassers could never escape. Vines of sharp thorns and blood red flowers covered the walls. It used to be that the flowers only bloomed when he was in the garden, but now they always bloomed because Juliana was there.

"Methought you would want to know about your brothers," he said. "I did my best to help them. I tried everything I could think of without risking Lucien knowing I looked for them. If he knew, I fear he might hurt them to hurt you, to hurt me. I could not bear that."

She didn't answer.

"But, Ean should be able to track them better than I, especially if he believes Thomas received no help from me in finding them. Though, I will continue to search for them. I have my goblins listening to the forest. I promise you, if there is anything I can do, I will do it."

Still, he received no answer from her.

"I was thinking of how unexpected it is that I would come to this spot to spy on you in the mortal realm, using Lucien's basin, and now I am once again forced to come here to see you and my child." He gave a small, unhappy laugh. "Even now, it would seem you obsess me, my queen."

He waited and, though he hoped, he still didn't get a response. It hardly surprised him. Juliana wasn't talking at all these days. Since his coronation as the Unblessed King, Merrick had watched his presence suck the life from the world around him. He was necessary, as necessary as light and spring. He was fall, winter, death to the land. Without him, the immortal world would not rest. Without him, good would not be. He knew this fact, had known it all his life. Only in Juliana had he realized his greatest fear—the fear that who he was would eventually suck the life from her as well.

"You said you would stand by me," he whispered, his tone mildly accusing. "You said you knew what you were doing, that I could not hurt you."

Finally he forced his gaze to the center platform to see her. His heart squeezed in his chest, as he stared at his wife's immobile face, frozen in the black stone prison she'd given herself. Her stomach was still rounded with their unborn child, cradled by one of her hands. Her other hand reached out, as it to take his.

The moment Merrick had seen what she had done, he'd moved her to his garden to protect her from the outside world. Naturally, some of his goblin subjects suspected what had happened, but they didn't care enough to pry into it. The creatures had no idea how long mortals were pregnant and the lack of a baby was not noticed.

None could know his pain. Merrick had to hide it. If his weakness was learned then war against Tegwen would be lost, his throne would be attacked and he'd lose any hope of seeing his Juliana again.

Merrick stepped up on the platform, taking her outstretched hand. He stood before her as if she were with him. Closing his eyes, he touched her stone hair and rested his chin on her head. "Why did you not tell me you were unhappy, Juliana? You seemed happy. I was happy with you." He took his hand from hers, sliding it up her arm to hug her tight. "Did my presence drain you, as it does everything else of beauty? Did you not want to tell me?"

He lifted his hand to her stomach, able to remember the feel of his child kicking at him. Now the stone didn't move, didn't answer his nearness or the call of his power. Was this his fate? To find her and lose her to this statuesque tomb? Was this a new torment for him, as the King of the Unblessed, to endure?

Merrick took a deep breath, able to imagine her free of stone. He could still hear her laugh, see her smile, taste her kiss. "Ah, my Juliana. Why did you not leave me a way to free you?"

# Chapter Six

*Tegwen Army Encampment, Mystic Forest*

"I already told your men. I am Sir Thomas of Bellemare, blessed ward to King Ean." Thomas sighed heavily, as he looked up from where he was tied to a tree. He sat on the ground. His legs sprawled before him, tied at the ankles, and his arms were bound back, stretched around the thick trunk.

A lot of good his escorts had been. The look Volos had given him most of the way could only be akin to a starving troll watching a walking feast. The large creature drooled constantly and, as the smaller Bevil whispered in his ear, both of them cackled sinisterly. Thomas barely slept the entire trip. After leading him over a glen of thorny bushes, past three sleeping dragons and through the mud pile of an unfriendly gnome, the two guides had finally abandoned him outside Tegwen's encampment. Unfortunately, it wasn't before they drew notice of half of the residing elfin army.

"What were you doing with King Merrick's men?" Commander Adal, leader of the Tegwen armies, was a big elf and one that seemed quite capable of leading his men.

The elfin soldiers were as tall and varied as humans, though they all appeared youthful and strong. There wasn't an old warrior amongst them. The only marked difference was the fashion of their clothing, their extremely long hair and the slight point to the tops of their ears. Most of the soldiers wore bright red tunics that hung long over their legs. They slit up the side to allow movement. Their dark breeches were plain and they wore boots, not unlike those worn in the mortal realm but for the odd pattern of embroidery.

"My sister is married to King Merrick and I visited her from the mortal realm. I was given the two guides to help me get here," Thomas answered.

"Well, at least you are not lying about your association with King Merrick," Adal said.

"I am not lying at all. Please, I seek an audience with King Ean. His wards, my brothers, have been taken. I believe Lucien has them."

Adal knelt down, facing him. "If you have not noticed, we are in the middle of a war. Why do you think the king would care about you and your brothers?"

"We are his blessed wards."

"Aye, so you have said."

"According to your scrolls, our line has continued to earn the blessing we have been given." Thomas was only repeating what Hugh had told him.

"We have been fighting a legion of dark elves for nearly a sennight. I lost good men and a horde of dragons have been spotted a two days ride from here, ensuring that I will lose even more. I expect they will attack by air tonight. What time do I have for reading scrolls?"

Thomas couldn't argue. What were the problems of his family to this man? To King Ean? Could he really expect the King of the Blessed to care about what happened to them? All because of some blessing the elf's father had given them a long time ago.

"I suppose I could spare one man to ride to where the king stays." Adal stood. "Until then, why do you not just rest right where you are at? If King Merrick sent you to spy on us, you will not be returning to report to him anytime soon."

Tania examined the faeries in her hall and they in turn stared back at her, their expressions solemn and pouting. Brooding, she sat on her throne, barely eating the meal set out before her on the long table. There was no music, no dancing, no laughter. She liked it that way. It fit her mood.

Her court had no problem making their displeasure of her change known. They were unhappy, because she was unhappy. She was the root of their magic and because she'd lost her innocence—no longer sacrificed the pleasure of her flesh—that magic was in limbo. Her purity was gone, the goodness inside her troubled and they all felt the effects. This should have been a happy day, the day their queen mated. But she didn't mate, merely lost a part of herself.

Why hadn't they bonded? She'd been willing. Hugh had made love to her. Under her breath, she said, "We made love. Why didn't he change? Why didn't I? Or was it just sin, not love?"

"Are you sure?" Lady Lily asked from the queen's side, revealing that she'd heard Tania's words. Her white wings didn't move as she sat on a chair. "Perchance you did not do it right."

Tania glanced up, surprised at the intrusion into her thoughts.

"And such is not a sin." Lady Roslyn leaned forward to look at her sister.

"It is if you're a queen," Lily said, "and he is not a faery king."

"It would make sense why he doesn't." Roslyn nodded thoughtfully.

"Why he is not." Lily pulled back her long blonde hair.

"Wait." Roslyn frowned. "Is he?"

Both sisters turned to look at her, expectant. Tania shook her head in denial. "Nay, he had not. He is the same stubborn earl."

"Are you sure you did it?" Lily eyed the dark markings on Tania's arms. She tried to be subtle about the inspection but the queen caught her.

Tania knew they were frightened by the change in her appearance.

"Are you going to go try it again?" Lily asked when Tania didn't speak. "Would you like us to go with you to make sure it is done right?"

Resentment rose within Tania. It was hard to control the new depth of emotions she felt. Just thinking of Hugh made her hurt, and anger was easier to feel than pain. How did other beings cope with such feelings? She thought of Lucien, tempted to summon him to take away the hurt. He could. The Damned King had that power and his offer was tempting. Besides, Lucien wasn't without his physical charms, his potent sexuality. He had offered to teach her sin, to take away her suffering. She'd lose her soul, but with it would go her conscience and surely then she wouldn't care.

"The earl is very handsome," Roslyn admitted. The hopeful look she gave her sister was not lost on the queen. "Would you like us to test him to make sure all his parts work correctly? He is human after all. Perchance he—"

"Nay. You will not touch him." Tania was well aware of how harsh she sounded. The idea of either one of them in Hugh's bed only furthered her temper.

"I think you should do it again," Lily advised. "And do not worry. We will be there to instruct you. No one will know. Then, ah," she looked at the queen's darkened hair, "this will all just..."

"Leave," Roslyn finished.

"Aye, and you will be your normal pretty self again," Lily said. "All this..."

"Darkness." Roslyn tried to be diplomatic.

"Aye, the darkness will just fade away," Lily finished. "And you will be beautiful once more, my queen."

Tania shot the faery a doleful glance before turning to silently stare at her depressed court once more.

Hugh wasn't sure how many days had passed since he'd been taken from Bellemare, but he knew he'd been at the faery palace for nearly four of them. Servants came, all male, to bring him clothes—a brown tunic and dark green pants. He fancied that he looked like a tree turned on its head. The material was light, hanging loose around his frame. Though comfortable, the fit was odd compared to the tighter breeches and layers of tunics he was used to. Along his back was a slit. It was clearly meant as an opening for wings.

The faery men brought food and instructed him to bathe in the bedchambers pool, going so far as to offer their help. Hugh had never in his life had a man bathe him and he wasn't about to start now—servant or not.

Why did his brother and Nicholas get pretty, willing females to tend them last they were here and all he got were males? Hugh frowned. It was hardly fair. Human women were often hard enough to understand, but faery women were impossible. Who knew what Tania was thinking? Her vanity and unstable temperament were evident in everything she did. Then why did she haunt him, filling his thoughts like she did?

Tania was never far from his mind. How could she be when he was trapped in her bedchambers? He tried to leave, only to hit an invisible barrier that he couldn't walk through. The other faeries could, but he was kept prisoner.

The queen did not visit him and he told himself he was glad for it, but his body liked to protest the fact. No matter how much his mind hated her, his body still desired her. The lust was primal, raw and on the verge of becoming painful.

"The servants tell me you requested to see me."

Hugh frowned, turning toward the entrance. Tania stood, her arms crossed, her face beautifully defiant. The dark coloring still affected her, but her eyes had cleared to their normal blue-gray color. For a moment, he couldn't speak as he looked at her clothing. In all his travels in the mortal realm, he'd never seen a gown like it. The black material covering her waist from breast to hips was cinched tight, held together with long strands of silk crossed up the front of the bodice. Beneath it, crimson red peeked through, lifting up to cover her breasts, though not so high he couldn't see the rounded tops. The skirt was ragged, as if cut by a knife, sliced over and over to fall in black strips. It only reached her knees. As she shifted her weight the black moved to show red underneath. Her feet and ankles were bare, but a cross lacing of red wound up her calves, disappearing up the skirt.

"Are you in a better temper, my lord?" she asked, when he

didn't speak.

"Let us see," he said, crossing his arms to match her stance. It took all his willpower not to be affected by her strange beauty. Though, there was a part of him that missed the lighter version he'd met a year ago. The queen had a purity about her then, which seemed to be gone now. "I have been held prisoner in this room. My brother is still missing. If I know Thomas he is wandering about in this realm alone, which means my lands are left unprotected at a very dire time. The future of Bellemare is under attack, its fate direr as each new foal dies. Oh, and you still have not told me what you want with me so I can only assume what I said last time we met was correct. You—"

"I did not take William." Tania looked hurt.

"That answers one of my questions," Hugh said. "That is, if I believed you. I have no reason to trust you."

She looked away. Was that guilt on her face?

"I know you were in bed with Lucien."

"I was not!" She gasped. "I have never taken that man to my bed. To do so would be a blemish on my soul. I will admit, I considered it, especially when you act so callous, but I never did."

"Let me rephrase." Hugh didn't like her admitting she'd thought of taking Lucien to her bed. Jealousy boiled at the very idea, and that jealousy only led to greater outrage. She was openly admitting she was in league with the demon. Even with her confession, part of him wanted to deny the truth of it. "I know you plotted with him to bring me here and I know his little helper was with William the last we saw him."

"Then Lucien has your brother, not I," Tania reasoned. "I only asked Lucien for you, to bring you here."

"You sent Lucien for us." Hugh took an aggressive step toward her, only stopping as he realized she stood by the door he couldn't pass through. If she ran away, it could be days before she came back. He didn't have the time to waste. "I do not wish to fight with you. I only wish to go. Tell me what it is you want from me, so that I may leave immediately."

She edged closer, her wings fluttered delicately behind her back. A sparkling of light shimmered from them. "Why must you go? This palace holds so many beauties, as does faery magic. Why face the cold, ugly world when you may have pleasure and happiness here?"

Hugh's eyes dipped over her body and it took all his control to concentrate on what he needed to do. He was well aware of the beauty and pleasures the faeries offered, and his body was more than willing to partake of them again. "I have responsibilities. They may not matter to you, but they are important to me. You brought me here. I would know why and I would know what I have to do to get my freedom so that I may leave."

"You said you would come back." Tania pouted her lower lip.

Hugh suppressed a groan. There was something about her that just stirred him. Magic, no doubt. Like those little bits of light that appeared from her wings. They were some kind of spell. He was sure of it.

"You said you would come back for me and you did not. You left to join the battle. I waited afterward for you, but you chose Bellemare." Her nose wrinkled. "You went there and did not come back. I do not think you were ever coming back."

Hugh stiffened, not moving. He'd run every conversation they'd had through his head several times over the last year. "Nay, I did not merely say that. I threatened to come back for you. I wanted to wring your neck for kidnapping me."

"I detained you, not kidnapped," she said. "Your sister's

story wasn't finished. She loved Merrick. I know, because I know love when I see it. She did. I will not let you confuse me again with your hateful words. Juliana was meant to be with him and I did the right thing in helping them be together."

Hugh wished he could believe that, but he'd seen Merrick's actions with his own eyes. The Unblessed King had told Juliana to go, had told her he didn't love her. Those were the facts.

"Fine, detained," he allowed. "But that does not change the fact that you hired the Damned King to take me because I did not come back to punish you for what you did to me."

"You did not say you were to punish me. You kissed me and you said you were coming back for me."

"So this is about sex." Hugh threw up his hands in frustration. "You had King Lucien kidnap me because I did not come back and copulate with you?"

This was too much. His house was attacked, his brother was gone, his life was turned upside down and all because this wench wanted him between her thighs. He knew he'd attracted his fair share of women, but this was almost too unbelievable.

She didn't meet his probing gaze. "Lucien was the only one with enough power to bring you here without drawing the notice of King Merrick or King Ean, but he was not supposed to hurt you. That was not part of the pact. I even made him promise not to hurt your family. He only agreed to a fortnight, but he did agree. So if he has William, your brother is unharmed for at least four more days. That is when the fortnight ends."

"If you wanted my sword inside you that badly..." He lowered his voice unintentionally as desire heated his blood. There was definitely something very alluring about a woman willing to go to such lengths just to sleep with him. "All you had to do was ask for it. You could have saved us both a lot of trouble."

"You mean to run me through?" She drifted closer, through the barrier of the door. "But you have no weapon."

Hugh laughed. How was it possible a faery, with all her supposed experience, was so naïve? He glanced down to where his erection pressed against his breeches. "I have weapon enough."

The moment his meaning finally dawned on her, he almost laughed. Her cheeks stained pink and her pretty little mouth fell open. More of the lights fell from her ashen wings.

Somehow not feeling as angry as he should, he crossed to her. Tania's big, blue eyes watched him as he lifted the crown off her head and put it aside, looping it over a potted flower on a nearby table. Turning back to her, he smoothed back her hair, running his fingers through it only to lift both sides up. He looked at the light and the dark together.

"There is much that I do not understand about this world," he said. "I do not understand magic. I do not understand the races who dwell here. But, most of all, I do not understand you, Queen Tania."

"I could teach you," she offered.

Hugh didn't have that kind of time. "I am sorry I did not come back for you. I did not know you took my threat as a promise. Had I known you waited for me, I just might have."

"Only might have?"

"Would you rather I lie to you?" He gave a small laugh when she shook her head in denial. "I was very angry with you for what you did. I still am. But, had I known you waited for me, aye, I just might have come back for you."

He stroked her soft, silken hair again. This time, as his hand ran over the darker half, her hair came from beneath his palm as the lighter blonde. Curious, he touched it again, running his fingers over the dark only to find that they had turned. He liked the natural color better and continued to touch her hair until it was all back to normal. Reaching for her cheek, he thought to wipe away the black line that was there. His finger traced it, but it didn't disappear.

"Then you accept being here?" she asked.

"I accept that I am here." Hugh didn't know what she was after. Was it just to take him as a lover? The attraction was there, he'd gone mad with it several times, but with no means to find her and ease the ache she caused. Had it been the same for her, until she was driven to find him? Was that all this game was—the need to fulfill their lust? "But, I need to find Thomas and William. Do you understand? I must see them."

"Aye."

Hugh was relieved. It could have gone much worse between them, but she was agreeing to let him go. In a way, her desire for him was sweet, no matter how misguided her actions were.

"Aye," he agreed with her as he turned her jaw to angle her mouth for a kiss. If the woman wanted him that badly, who was he to deny her one last time before he left? If what she said was true, then William was safe for the time being. After he left her, he'd find Thomas and together they'd meet with King Ean to get William back. Then, they'd call on Juliana to make sure she was safe and offer again for her to come home. Her half elfin child would naturally be welcome, despite the fact that Hugh was fearful of what powers the baby might possess. He smiled against Tania's mouth. Within a sennight, his family could be back together as it should be—all safe and sound at Bellemare and out of the realm of magic forever.

Tania met the earl's lips. If all he wanted was to find where his brothers were at, he should have just asked. She'd taken strands of their hair as well the last time they were at her palace and with the help of the divination pool, she could locate them easily for him.

But, instead he'd just gotten mad and yelled, hurting her feelings. It only proved that mortals' moods could be very changeable. They were quick to anger, quick to passion, quick to happiness. Perchance it was their mortality that made them that way. It would make sense. Humans didn't live long and they had to fit a lot of things into such a short amount of time. That would also account for why they were always in a hurry.

Tania had spied on copulating mortals and knew the ways of lovemaking between men and women, and still she was surprised when Hugh didn't carry her off to the bed. Instead, his hands pulled at her bodice, freeing her breasts from the lighter red material. The tight black corset around her waist didn't budge. Her wings fluttered in pleasure and her feet lifted off the floor. Hugh growled, pulling her back down by her hips.

His gaze hot with passion, he pushed her against an uneven wall and leaned over to take a nipple into his mouth. Her flesh glistened with pleasure, sparkling in the diffused light coming through the crystal-like walls. His kisses were angry, though she didn't get the impression he was mad.

"Part your thighs." He stripped from his tunic before falling to his knees. He didn't give her time to answer as he lifted her skirt out of his way, disappearing beneath it. Her leg was thrust over his naked shoulder. The earl gripped her ass, pulling her sex to his mouth. She gasped at the wet, hot feeling of his probing tongue. Tania wiggled and his grip tightened.

"Hugh?" Her legs weak, the tension within her built. She tapped his head beneath her skirt. "Hugh?"

He made a grumbling noise, while fighting his way out from underneath the material. Pulling back, he looked up at her. "Aye?"

"Should we not?" She motioned toward the bed.

Hugh surged to his feet. "Mmm, nay, here is good."

He kissed her hard, stealing her breath. Before she could again focus her thoughts, his breeches were around his feet, her skirt was pushed up and he was lifting her up along the wall. He entered her with a confident thrust. His face buried in her chest as he held her before him. Tania held on, surprised by the rough, mindless way his body thrust inside hers. The tension built anew and she welcomed it, feeling the power of release feeding her magic. The sensation was like an enchantment and she could see why the faeries of her court couldn't resist its call. She felt powerful and alive. Pheromones sprinkled them as they exploded off her body, wrapping them in a cocoon of pleasure. Hugh grunted, making the noises that men made at such moments. Suddenly, she came, gripping onto him as her whole body shook. Hugh was soon to follow, burying himself deep inside her as he met with release.

After, he slowly lowered her to the floor, breathing hard as he kept her against the wall. Tania wrapped her arms around him, lifting them up. He glanced at her in surprise as she pulled his great weight off the floor, flying them to the bed. Landing on the mattress, she urged him to lay with her. As her bodice disappeared, coverlets appeared over them. Hugh held her close, his eyes closed.

"Did you want me to bring you to look for them?" she asked, empowered and not at all tired.

He mumbled against her skin.

"Hugh, did you want to look?"

"Mmm, nay, I want to lay here and relax," he answered sleepily. "I will look later."

Tania smiled happily, holding him while he went to sleep. Running her hands over his back, she frowned to feel the flat surface. Why didn't he change yet? Their bond was complete. Wasn't it?

Her smile faded as she thought of Lily and Roslyn. Did they know something she didn't? Was there something she was missing? She didn't want to bring the women in with her, was repulsed by the very idea of sharing, but if Hugh didn't change soon she might not have a choice.

"Giants be big and piskies be small, but that no' affect the bedsport at all," William sang, utterly bored and out of spells. The song sounded much better after a night of drinking piskie ale.

Without his wand, he couldn't create a spell to get out of his chains and he couldn't call his fellow wizards for help. Too bad he hadn't been carrying the thing on him when the lovely maid captured him. The wand was back at Bellemare, hidden in his bedchambers.

William sighed. Here he was in the immortal realm and he couldn't even partake of any of his normal amusements. Being a wizard, he knew how to sense the magic around him. Wherever he was, it was a powerful place.

"What do you say, good sirs?" William asked his lethargic companions. "Shall we go have a pint after we get out of here?"

As predicted, he didn't get an answer.

"Last one to say 'aye' buys," William said. "Aye."

Again, nothing.

"Ah, well then, I will happily take a pint from each of you. Mighty generous, good sirs, mighty generous." William sighed heavily. "So, what crime got you—?"

Hearing a whooshing noise breaking into the silence he'd grown accustomed to in the prison, he instantly dropped his head, pretending to be like his unmoving companions. His hair stirred about his head, giving him a chill.

"I heard you singing," a woman's voice said.

William opened one eye to look. The violet-eyed kidnapper stared back at him, surrounded by the soft green light of a short distance portal. He easily concluded that the portal was the door to the chamber. The woman wore a long, black cloak to hide her figure. The material was big, as if it didn't belong to her. "For a mercenary, you are very attractive."

"For a prisoner, you are very alert," she said.

"My companions and I have been getting along magnificently." William tilted his head toward the side, motioning to the three men. "They cannot sing worth a spell, but we are working on it."

"Come, we do not have much time. He will sense I am gone," the woman said.

"He? Who is he?" William asked as she knelt before him to pull at the chains binding his ankles. He watched as she scraped her nail across one manacle. It clicked open. "And for that matter, who are you?"

"I am Mia," she answered, opening the second in the same fashion, only using a different nail. "And the he is King Lucien."

"I do not understand. You came to Bellemare to warn me about Lucien. Then you kidnapped me and brought me to Lucien and now..." William paused, instantly distracted as she stood before him. Her cloak parted and he saw that she wore hardly a stitch of clothing except for a ring of leather bands that wrapped along her body, winding from her shoulders to her thighs like a very lucky snake. He grinned, staring as he slowly finished, "And now you wish to free me."

"I did not kidnap you," she whispered, liberating a wrist. "And keep your voice down. We do not have much time."

"If this is Lucien's prison, where did you get the magic to free me?"

Mia cursed, as she scraped her fingernail and the manacle didn't open. She moved to a pinkie, doing it again. The manacle gave way, but William was still stuck on the wall. He flailed about, his arms and legs kicking as he was held by his back. She pushed him over, so his face was directed at his prone elfin friend.

"Hold on, we need to lift you up. Your breeches are hooked," she said.

"Methought they were a bit snug. Done gone up the crac—"

"Got it." She pushed him up only to set him down hard on the stone floor.

"Ow, take it easy." William wiggled, shaking his hands while trying to free his breeches from where they'd traveled up. "My limbs are numb and my backside aches. And, to tell the truth of it, I think I have got a bruise or two."

"Come, you must go. There is not much time. He might already know I have come to free you."

"But what about my friends here." William pointed over his shoulder. "They owe me a pint. I cannot leave them behind to rot."

"There is no time for playing hero. If you are gone, it will be excused as your wizard magic. If they are gone, he will know I helped you."

"By the by, how are you helping me? If you have enough magic to break in here, you should not fear Lucien. What manner of creature are you, anyway."

Mia held up her hands. "Skin from the Damned King's

back. I kept it under my nails. And when I put my lips to you that was his dried blood."

"Methought your lips looked pinker today," William observed.

"Do you want to die? We do not have time for this. You must leave. Now." She tried to grab his arm.

"You never said what you were."

"A nymph. Now please, you have to leave. I promise to find a way to free them later."

William turned to bow to the three prisoners in farewell. Before the words could leave him, he stiffened in surprise. "Sir Nicholas? He is alive? How is this possible? Hugh said he saw him die."

William rushed to the man. Nicholas' flesh was grayer than a mortal's should've been. His cheeks were sunken in, making his eye sockets protrude. His brown hair hung long around his head, uneven and stringy, just like his beard.

"Mia, help me to free him now. I cannot leave him here," William said.

"Do you not care that we could be caught and this is your only chance at escape? I do not think I can make it here in time to save you again. Lucien plans to kill you in two days."

"You know, I do not really get panicked. Apprentice wizards cast a spell over themselves to take away panic and fear, so that we may bravely face anything. Though, I did give it to myself three times. I did not think I had it right. Turns out, I did. And, I must say, it does help the confidence with the fair maids." He winked at her.

Mia shook her head with a small sound of exasperation. "Great. Of all the wizards, I get stuck rescuing one who does not have any sense."

"Who are these two?" He looked at the elves. They looked familiar, but in truth all elves tended to look the same to him.

"I do not know." She tried to pull his arm. "Come."

"I am not leaving without them. By my wizard's honor, I cannot—"

"Fine," Mia huffed, crossing over to Nicholas. "But know that as you save them, you most assuredly condemn me."

"I will protect you," William swore. "You have nothing to fear."

She gave a short laugh, but didn't respond. Mia scraped at her nails, taking several tries to free Nicholas of his manacles. "He is going to be disoriented at first. It has been a long time for him in here. After that, just pray he does not still carry a demon inside him. Even if he does not, Lucien's had him trapped in a personal hell. He will be a changed man."

"I will be sure to watch my back." As William pushed Nicholas up to get him unhooked, he nodded at the other two. "Now them."

"I cannot."

"They are blessed elves," William said. "I can tell that much. And if they are in here, they are in trouble. We cannot leave them behind."

"But—" Mia glanced at the green portal. She looked scared. Then, as if coming to a decision, she nodded. "Let us hope some of his blood lingers."

"Do I even want to know how you got close enough to the Damned King to get his blood and flesh?" William asked. The look she shot him was answer enough. He shivered, suddenly feeling very sorry for the woman and what she risked. The emotion kicked him out of his spell-induced stupor and made his heart beat faster. It had been a long time since he'd felt apprehension and he didn't like it. But, knowing that she was scared made him scared as well.

Licking her lips, she went across to the ankles, kissing the manacles. The metal creaked open, but barely. Then, telling William to give her a boost up, she did the same along the top, but the magic wore out and she couldn't get the last wrist manacle to open. She licked her lips again, trying several times. William set her down and she used her nails. It wouldn't open.

"I cannot," she said. "The magic is gone. I used it all up."

William looked at the poor elf in pity as he helped the one they could free off the wall. The two men didn't move. William slapped their face several times. Still nothing.

"Listen to me." Mia reached within her cloak. Her hand came back with a vial. "I have a portal here that will take you to Feia. Your brother Hugh is there. He is being held prisoner by Queen Tania. This is the most I can help you. Once there, you will have to free yourself from the faeries. Just try not to get any of their pheromones on you."

"Again?" William asked, surprised. "Hugh is trapped by Queen Tania again?"

"She made a deal with Lucien to get him back. I do not know why exactly, though I think it is because she wanted him as a lover, needs him as a lover to take her maidenhead? I am not sure on that point. I never did learn much about faeries. All I know is if Tania succeeds in whatever it is she plans, the earl will never return home. He will be trapped here in this realm. Forever."

"Just tell me this after we get out of here. There will be plenty of time once—"

Mia threw the vial, stopping his words. A white, swirling portal opened. Grabbing the elf by the arm, she dragged him toward it, pushing him in. The portal grabbed him in its vortex, pulling him through with a gust of wind. Mia's hair stretched toward it, but she kept back far enough not to get pulled in as she went for Sir Nicholas.

William helped her drag the man to the portal and they shoved him in. "Are you ready?"

"I cannot go with you."

"But you said he would be angry about this," William protested. "Do not worry. I'll explain everything to my brother. He will understand and will not be angry. Come to Bellemare with us. We will keep you safe."

She smiled sadly and came toward him as if to hug him. William held out his arms, ready to feel her soft body against him. Suddenly, she ducked, pushing him through the portal. He gasped in surprise as he was helplessly sucked into the churning center.

"Mia." He tried to yell, but the word was lost in the heavy winds.

Mia stood on the other side, her hand lifting up in farewell. Her image grew fainter as he was pulled away from the Damned King's dungeon. The remaining elf prisoner's free limbs reached forward as if he would come too, but the manacle held him back. The portal dimmed and he knew Mia closed it on her side, staying behind to face whatever punishment Lucien dealt her.

Lucien lounged before his fireplace, watching Mia's deceit unfold on his bedchamber floor. The flames moved like a life size fire play, mimicking the people in his dungeon. He'd known that Mia would try something, had expected her to, but still her betrayal angered him.

Why couldn't he command her loyalty to him? Why did she have to fight him so? Even as he craved her complete submission, he longed for her defiant nature.

He watched, his chest tight with uneasiness, as he waited to see if she would again kiss William. He heard their words in his head, even as the fire showed their actions. Finally, she pushed William through the portal she'd stolen from him—the one he'd let her take.

The hold on his chest eased. She hadn't kissed the wizard, but she did save his life, sending one of his most prized prisoners with him—Prince Ladon of Tegwen.

Lifting his hand, he balled it into a fist to extinguish the flames. He could've stopped her at any moment, kept his prisoners, but he wanted William to cause trouble between Queen Tania and the earl. Mia's rescue scheme did just that. He'd lied to Mia about Tania's intentions, purposefully told her of William's capture, all the while knowing she'd free the wizard and tell him of Hugh's imprisonment. He predicted she might free Sir Nicholas, but he hadn't anticipated her having enough of his magic leftover to free the elf prince as well. At least he still had one Tegwen prince left to him.

Prince Ladon had spent over fifty years in his prison, plagued by evil thoughts. It would only be a matter of time before those thoughts took hold inside him—creeping into his dreams, into his actions, into his temperament. It wouldn't be foreseeable, not like if he carried a demon inside of him. Ladon would fall into darkness harder than his brother, Merrick. And if Ladon failed to succumb, Lucien always had Wolfe.

Lucien wasn't concerned with Nicholas. The man was weak and it took less than a year to break his spirit fully. After he took in the demon and killed his own father, Nicholas' soul had been half dead anyway. Now, he was merely a pawn that Lucien would use to prey upon the Bellemare family's goodness. He saw many scenarios with Nicholas and the Bellemares. If Nicholas made it back to the mortal world, he would carry his demon with him. If he didn't, he would either haunt the Bellemare family with his absence or would show them just how powerful Lucien's demons were and haunt them with their fear. Any way it happened, Nicholas served a meager purpose.

With barely any concentration, he willed that Ladon and Nicholas should awaken from their troubled sleeps. He also willed that they stayed weak and disorientated, at least for the time being. Let William the Wizard split Tania from her lover first. He glanced at the bed, seeing the faery queen's image in the sudden flames. Her powers were still weakened, closer to darkness than to light. It allowed him to spy on her without her knowing. Hugh was with her and there was no mistaking the status of her former maidenhead.

"Where have you been?" He squelched the fire as Mia slipped into the room. "I woke up and you were gone."

"Wandering the halls," Mia answered. "I could not sleep and did not wish to disturb you."

He hid his rueful smile, keeping his face blank as she lied to him. "Always the thoughtful one, are you not, sweet nymph?"

# Chapter Seven

Hugh was trapped in the euphoria of Tania's embrace. He couldn't stop touching her, couldn't keep from making love to her whenever she was near. The few times she did leave him, he waited breathlessly for her to come back. Nothing else mattered. Nothing existed beyond her body, her voice, her kiss. When he closed his eyes, it was to think of her. And each time they came together, the euphoria thickened as did his pleasure. He'd never felt so free in his life—free of responsibility, of thought, of duty. There was only Queen Tania and he couldn't get enough of her.

Blinking as he became fully awake, he automatically reached for her. His shaft was hard, ready to again feel her body on his. Already they'd made love all over her bedchambers—in the bathing pool surrounded by vines, on the hard floor, on the soft bed, against the wall—and in every position imaginable.

His hands met with an empty bed. Frowning, he looked around the room for her.

"Tania?" He sat up on the mattress. "Tania, come to bed."

Sensing she was near, he looked at the door to the bedchamber, eager to see what she'd be wearing today. The lines on her body didn't fade, but her hair stayed the same honeyed blonde. She always heard when he called and, since he had taken her against the wall, she always came to him when he beckoned.

Her midriff was bare, showing between a short, tattered gray and green skirt and a bodice that only covered her breasts. A wreath of vines twirled in place of her normal silver crown. As always, her hair flowed about her shoulders and her wings flapped behind her as they carried her forward. Her long legs were still as they drifted through the air. She didn't wear shoes upon her feet, leaving them bare.

Hugh stared at her toes, groaning in arousal. Every inch of her turned him on. His gaze traveled up her legs, to where her thighs were exposed, her sex barely covered with the skirt. Part of him wanted to say something about her going around her palace in such revealing attire, but the thought slipped away as soon as he had it. He continued his visual journey up to her tight stomach. The skirt was low enough to show her navel. The practically non-existent top clung to her chest, held on by one strap across her shoulder, while giving him the impression of budded nipples.

"Hugh, we have visitors outside the palace," Tania said. "You should dress and come down from the tower."

"Come to bed." He did not care if fifty kings awaited his appearance.

"You spend all day in here."

"I do not hear you complaining while you are in it." He stood. Reaching over to swipe her foot, he grabbed her and pulled her down next to him. Instantly his lips were on her neck, kissing her. She moaned, responding like she always did. Each time he wanted her, he found her body wet and ready for him, her desires enough to match his own.

Running his hands along her waist, he pushed her top up to find her nipples were indeed hard. Hugh captured one in his mouth, mindlessly sucking and biting it. The small, pretty sounds she made turned him on more. Her magic fell over him in tiny dots of light, impassioning him even more. Like a man starved for release, he caressed her legs, impatiently pulling up her skirt to find her naked ass and hips. Her small hand wrapped around his arousal, stroking it so lightly that it made him ache for her tight sheath.

Her skin was so soft, so warm and he knew she'd fit tightly over his erection. Hugh dipped his finger into the cream of her body, rubbing her clit as he parted her folds. Unable to resist, he slipped a finger inside, moving within her sex so it trembled and squeezed him.

"Do you want me to tell you about the visitors?" she asked, breathless. "William is with them."

*William? William who?*

Hugh merely groaned, sucking her chest harder. He loved her breasts, wanted to spend an eternity with them firmly in his mouth.

"Your brother, William." Her voice was so soft it sounded like far off bells.

"He'll wait." Hugh grunted, not thinking beyond her taste. "I will not."

Brusquely, he pushed her to the side, making her fall onto her hands. Maneuvering her light body, he grabbed her hips and angled her ass toward him. Hugh pushed her skirt up so he could look at her.

Tania's wings fluttered before his face, stirring the air so it tickled his flesh. He pushed her legs open. Need pumped through him, centering in his loins. He needed her. Now.

Guiding himself to her sex, he eased the tip of his shaft inside her warm depths. It felt so good, like she was tightly carved just for his shape. He pulled her back, watching himself move within her. Tania's wings flapped harder, sprinkling them with more magic. He was learning to read her responses and knew she found as much pleasure as he.

Pushing deep, he then withdrew, only to plunge in once more. He controlled her with her hips, riding her, moving in and out, in and out, watching the scandalously captivating display of his glistening member soaked by her body's moisture.

Tania reached between her thighs and he felt her tighten over him. It was like this each time, their bodies completely in sync, climaxing in unison. The tension built until he was desperate to spill his seed. Gasping, he clutched her to him, finding his release. Tania's cry joined his. For a brief moment, he held still, basking in the feelings before finally collapsing next to her on the bed.

Tania rolled off the bed. After they came together, she always appeared energetic when he just wanted to rest. Humming softly, she crossed to the bathing pool. Her clothes disappeared as she stepped in. His body stirring anew, he pushed up and made a move to follow her. By the time he got there, she'd turned around and was stepping out. Her body dried instantly, glistening with oils as a new outfit appeared. This one was tight from shoulder to hip with a skirt that flared to the floor. A breeze stirred and the hair at her temples pushed up on her head. The vine headpiece disappeared and was replaced by the silver crown.

"Rinse off and come with me to the hall," she said. "The faeries would like to see you are alive. I promised them that you would come down today."

He started to answer, only to frown as he stepped into the pool. Had he not left the room? Hugh tried to remember, but couldn't. All he could think about was his queen.

"I've put clothes for you on the bed," she said as he stepped out, dripping wet. She blew a kiss at him and the moisture on his body dried, sending a chill over his length. Tania flew above his reach as he crossed to the bed. Seeing a folded outfit where he'd been sleeping moments before, he pulled the dark green tunic over his head and tugged on the breeches. There weren't any shoes, but he didn't care. Tania was at the door, motioning to him. Mindless, he followed her, unable to take his eyes from her. If she flew off the top of the palace, he'd gladly step after her even though he had no wings.

William glanced around, not seeing the faery palace. He knew it was hidden in the woods, but Mia's portal took him to its hiding spot, not to the palace. Turning to the two men on the ground, he frowned. They had awakened, but were dazed, their eyes bloodshot as they looked around in confusion. Sir Nicholas didn't even know his name, or not so much that he knew to answer to it.

Kicking at the ground, William looked for a faery ring. The cluster of mushrooms and darker grasses would let him gain entrance into the Silver Palace, or at least it would in theory. As he wasn't well-versed in reading faery rings, he supposed they could lead to other places as well. But, where there was a ring, normally could be found a faery crossing through it. Then, all he'd have to do was charm the little winged beauty and he'd gain audience with the queen.

Suddenly, flakes of silver light drifted around him and he looked up. They fell down from the heavens. The warm sparks hit his flesh. He listened, hearing the song of the faeries in the wind—the sound of rustling leaves high in the trees.

"Ah, Queen Tania." William knew the faery queen was showing him the way. But why, if she thought to trap his brother? William knew enough of the immortal realm not to take things as they appeared. Mia had saved him, but she'd also trapped him. Did she stay behind as a martyr because she knew Lucien wouldn't harm her? Or did he follow his instincts and believe her? Or were his instincts too readily bound to his lustful passions?

There were too many questions to be answered at the moment. He would have to listen and watch, seeing Tania and Hugh together. It was no secret amongst Thomas and William that Hugh obsessed over the faery. Perchance it was time to see where that obsession would lead the earl.

Tania tried not to turn around to look at Hugh as she entered the hall. He followed behind her. She could feel his eyes looking at her—hot, passionate. The man was insatiable. It wasn't a bad thing, for her desire ran just as molten, but there was a time and place for such things. In the passageway right outside her great hall wasn't one of them.

Each time they made love, the palace began to brighten—not so much as before, but the silver walls were no longer tarnished and rusted. The dark lines on her body hadn't lessened, but her wings were not as gray and her hair had returned to normal. That was something. It gave her hope. And they were happy, right? He seemed happy. Hugh didn't yell at her like when he'd first arrived.

"I will let William in." She entered the palace hall and willed the palace to appear before William so that he may find the front gate. "Whispers came from the forest about your brother appearing. He comes with two men, but I cannot tell who they are."

"Come here," Hugh said and she felt his hand on her hip. "I want to talk to you."

"Talk?" she laughed in disbelief.

"Aye, among other things," he said naughtily.

"My lord, have you been listening? William is not a prisoner of Lucien. He is safe." She frowned. Somehow, she'd assumed the news would have pleased him, but he didn't seem to be concerned. That wasn't like Hugh not to care. Normally, he cared a great deal about a great many things. "You were worried about your brother and now he is here, safe."

"Excellent." Hugh sighed, but she got the impression he wasn't really listening. "Let us go back to bed."

Tania pushed his hand from her hip, even as pheromones erupted from her wings, attesting to her bodily interest in his offer. "Methought you wanted to talk."

"Wed with me. Be my wife." Hugh again reached for her. Tania's mouth opened in surprise. Pleasure unfurled within her as she began to nod. Only, a sobering voice broke into her answer before she could speak it.

"Hugh?"

Tania turned toward the hall. A few faeries flew overhead. William entered, holding the hands of his two companions. Tania ignored the men, as she watched William. He let go and they stopped walking, standing completely still in the entryway. Seeing the earl, William strode forward.

"Hugh," William demanded.

"Aye?" Hugh did not turn to him.

"Hugh," William said, louder as he went to his brother. He shot Tania an irritated glance before taking Hugh by the shoulders and forcibly turning him around. "Hugh, look me in the eyes."

Tania stepped back, frowning. Hugh gazed at his brother, but his face was blank. William let go of him, turning to the queen.

"You drugged him," William accused.

Tania gasped, the sound joined by her subjects in her hall. More had gathered to see the palace guests. "I have not!"

William glared at her and she shook her head. What was he talking about? Drugged? She'd not done anything to him—well aside from the slight "detainment". Oh, and the small matter with King Lucien. Guiltily, she looked away.

"Hugh!" William yelled and she couldn't resist glancing back to see what was happening. "Hugh, see me!"

"He can see you. He is looking directly at you," Tania said.

"Do you not see it?" William demanded, not sounding as angry at her as before. "Look at his eyes. They are dazed."

"Ah...?" She frowned. He didn't look any different to her. Hugh's face turned to her and he smiled, the come-hither look in his eyes as if he beckoned her to his bed. Tania shivered, drawn forward to answer his call.

"Oh, really? Then observe." William drew back his hand and slapped Hugh across the face. The earl grunted, blinking as he turned to look at his brother. William slapped him again.

"William?" Hugh blinked in bewilderment.

Tania flew forward, reaching to protect him. Hugh turned to her, drawing back slightly from her touch.

"What is happening?" Hugh asked, shaking his head. Then, as if finally feeling the pain of William's slap, he grunted and reached for his face. "Did you hit me?"

"Aye," William nodded. "And a good thing I did, too."

"Blessed saints!" Hugh rubbed his cheek, confused. "William, why did you...?" Stopping, his eyes rounded.

"William? By all that is holy, it is you!" He grabbed his brother, pulling him into a fierce hug as he pounded his brother's back. "How did you get here? Methought Lucien had you. I..."

"Lucien did have me. The violet-eyed nymph, her name is Mia by the by. She freed me and sent me to you." William returned the embrace as Hugh pounded him on the back a couple of times. "Actually, she detained me at Bellemare and then I woke up in Lucien's hold. I'm not sure how I got there or if she did it, but she did free me. She claims Lucien was going to kill me in two days."

"Two days?" Hugh whispered, his voice anguished. "Wait, Mia. I know that name. She took me to the Fire Palace and then begged Lucien not to hurt me. That is the violet-eyed woman? She is working for King Lucien."

"I think she is forced to help him," William said. "She tried to warn me at Bellemare about Lucien and she did save my life."

"She takes us to save us?" Hugh frowned. "I do not trust her. I do not trust any women of this realm."

Tania's stomach knotted in fear as she watched the interplay. The answer to his question burned inside of her, only how could she give it to him now. How things had changed in a single flap of her wings! Slowly, Hugh turned to her and she felt as if her world was ending. His eyes were hard, so unlike moments before. There was no love in him, not for her, not for anything at the moment.

"I was going to go get you," Hugh continued to his brother, his voice tight as he looked at her. "I was going to leave days ago to find you."

"Hugh, I..." Tania tried to speak. When William slapped his brother's face, her head had cleared some. Lightly, she whispered, trying to explain what had happened to him,

"Euphoria."

"Do not you say a single word to me!" Hugh demanded. "No more of your faery spells. I cannot believe you did it to me again. You drugged me to keep me here. You took away my will."

"I did not," she said weakly. "I swear to you, Hugh. If I did, I did not know."

Why hadn't she seen it? Hugh had been drugged with faery passion. Though, she'd never put a man under her spell, she had see it before, many times. She should have seen that Hugh was under faery magic. Did that mean the last couple of days were a lie? She'd been a fool. She hadn't wanted to see the truth.

"You do not love me," she whispered, shaking her head. A severe pain etched itself over her. She felt her scalp burning and lifted a hand to touch her head. Strands of her hair fell forward as she lowered her chin. They were again dark. The walls of the palace began to tarnish once more, evidence of the lie their time had been. Her faeries made weak noises as they began murmuring frantically amongst themselves.

"Not anymore," Hugh growled. "Not that you could call what happened to me love. Your spell is broken."

Tania sunk to the ground, too weak to fly. Her wings drooped and she had to put a hand on the chilly floor to keep from falling over. Inside she felt cold, alone. Had the euphoria impaired her as well? Was she awakening from a dream into bitter reality?

Hugh towered above her, his feet stopping near her hand. Her whole body shook. She wanted to reach for him, but couldn't move more than a finger toward his shoe.

"You selfish woman," he hissed. "Is my life some sort of diversion to you? First Juliana and now you almost cost me

William. You are fortunate you are a woman otherwise you would be dead right now for all you have done to my family. But, if your antics have in anyway harmed Thomas, I will be back to settle. And make no mistake, this time it will not be to take you to bed, but to kill you—and your being a woman will not stay my hand."

The faeries in her hall gasped at his declaration. She felt their eyes on her, knew they were confused, scared. For the first time since her reign, she didn't think she could protect them. She was drained, tired, and she was too weak to stop him from going.

"You are leaving?" She hoped by some miracle he would stay.

"Oh, aye, most certainly. I am done with this place, this realm of magic and I am done with you, Queen Tania. If I never see you again, it will be too soon. I am going home to Bellemare and I am taking all my family with me—all of my family."

"Nay." She shook her head, trying to form the words she needed to speak. It was hard under the stare of his accusing rage. "You cannot."

"Pardon me?" he demanded.

"You cannot go. You will die if you go back to Bellemare."

"You are threatening to kill me if I leave?" Hugh snorted in obvious disbelief. "Farewell, Tania."

"Nay, wait." She tried to make him understand.

"Come, William." Hugh turned his back on her. "Let us get out of this accursed place."

"Nay, Hugh." Tania pushed up from the floor. Her limbs shook and she couldn't move her wings.

He didn't stop walking.

"Hugh, please." Tears streamed down her face. Tania fell

back down, resting against the hard stone. "Please do not leave me. I love you. I want to wed with you. Please, Hugh, just love me."

✧

"I would apologize for my commander's hospitality, but we are in the middle of the war. You were seen with goblins and there was no way for him to know if you were who you said you were."

"I understand," Thomas said, trying to stretch his sore muscles as he looked at King Ean. He'd been treated fairly, considering the entire encampment had been busy with other things. The elves had fed him, gave him a fire, let him stretch his legs regularly. They took his sword, but hadn't searched him for other weapons, a thing he found odd, but excused as them being unafraid of any human defense he'd be capable of. "Commander Adal and I have never been introduced. I did not expect that he would know me."

King Ean sat on the floor of the white gossamer tent. The walls were transparent, allowing them to see the small encampment in the forest and the elfin army that inhabited it. However, all sound was blocked, like they were surrounded by thick, impenetrable stone.

Threads of gold shone with daylight along the tent walls, reflecting the sun. The king was the only other person with him, completely unprotected in his red tunic. It was the same design as his men, only it was embroidered with blue instead of gold. Just like the last time he'd been in the king's presence, Thomas felt a strange connection to the man. It was more of a pull, a sensation of the familiar, like when he was near his brothers, or his father before he died. Hugh said being near the Blessed

King reminded him of the feeling he got in the moment of winning a tournament or battle. Whatever it was, the feeling was nearly impossible to describe and Thomas was inclined to think that one could only understand if they'd felt it for themselves. But, regardless, the connection was there.

"I do not think you do understand," Ean said. "It is not that Adal did not know who you might be, but that he was not sure you were not a shapechanger. Rumors have come from the forest order of wizards that Merrick has conjured the power to create one.

"One what?"

"A shapechanger," Ean repeated. Blond hair hung long around his shoulders, very much like King Merrick's, but instead of the darkness of the Unblessed King's eyes, Ean's were blue. "You were seen being escorted by a goblin and a troll toward my encampment only to be left alone by them before trying to make yourself known. Trolls and humans are rarely seen together. It would take a great act to create such a circumstance—say the will of the Unblessed King. It was feared Merrick sent a spy into our midst."

"I am no spy. I did go to Merrick's castle, but only because my sister is there, or was there. I am only in this realm to find my brothers." Thomas sighed. "And, apparently, my sister now as well."

"It would seem your family cannot stay away from this realm," Ean mused.

"It would appear so." Thomas nodded. "But I assure you, it has not been from lack of trying."

Standing gracefully, the king faced Thomas. "You went to the Black Palace?"

"Aye."

"And Juliana was not there?"

"Not that I could see."

"Merrick did not explain her absence?"

"He said she was in the garden and would not come out. I know my sister. Juliana would not refuse to see me, not after so long apart. King Merrick is hiding her from me and deliberately not telling me what I would know. I was hoping you might know something."

"Of the Unblessed Queen?" Ean shook his head. "Nay. None have seen her. We listen for news of an heir, but..."

"What?" His stomach tightened. He had the sick feeling something happened to Juliana. It had been so long since he'd seen her, not counting the old magical missive he'd watched, and Merrick was refusing to let him talk to her. "Please, tell me. What is it?"

"Merrick should not be able to have a child. I fear the baby might not be his."

"Nay," Thomas instantly denied, ready to defend his sister's honor. "Juliana would never—"

Ean held up his hand. "I do not mean to upset you, Sir Thomas. I only mean to tell you the truth." He motioned around them to the tent walls. "This is a place of truth. If either of us were to lie, the walls would collapse upon us."

Thomas nodded, remembering Hugh describing the tent as such a place. "Please, what do you know of my sister? Can you feel anything? She is one of your wards."

"I know nothing of your sister. As the Unblessed Queen, she is no longer my ward. She belongs to Merrick."

"I want to see her, but he will not let me talk to her. I do not know how to reach her. I—"

"I know nothing of your sister," Ean repeated, cutting him off, "but I do know my realm."

"And your brother? You do know him, right? Merrick..." Thomas didn't continue. The king's eyes turned away from him. "I apologize."

"King Merrick was once my brother, but those ties have been..." Ean took a deep breath, closing his eyes. "It is not as it once was. Times have changed. Fate has seen to that."

"The bonds of blood can never be severed." Thomas wasn't sure if he was helping. He only knew no matter what happened, he would never give up on his family. They were a part of him, a part of his soul and such ties could never be broken.

"That is easy for humans to believe, but an eternity is so much longer than a human lifetime. To you a day is precious, yet to us it is a blur amongst a hundred more like it. You think a year a long time, I think it a blink." Ean patted his arm. "You cannot know what an eternity can do to the bonds of blood. How many centuries does a man hold on after the ties are strained? I can tell you what the Merrick of my youth would have done, but King Merrick of the Unblessed? Nay, I cannot tell you what deceits he is capable of, only that none of his deceits would surprise me. The Merrick of my youth would never have started this war, yet now, he is the first to shoot the arrow."

Thomas didn't answer. Inside, he wanted to scream in frustration. He just wanted his family back. Still, he got the feeling that, on some level, Ean felt as frustrated as he did, as alone and tired.

"It is hard enough for elves to beget heirs, but for King Merrick it should have been impossible. He is unblessed and heirs are a blessing. The very idea that Juliana carries his child contradicts that truth. But, if by some black magic or by some strange will, she does carry his child, I fear the outcome cannot be a happy one." Ean sighed. "I am sorry to have to tell you this, but Juliana might be lost to you."

"Nay, I..." Thomas paused, thinking of Hugh and his suspicions of the Unblessed King. Thomas was beginning to agree with him. He didn't for a moment think Juliana would carry any but Merrick's child. That didn't bode well though. What if merely carrying the baby killed her? What if Merrick's seed changed her, harmed her? Begetting children was risky enough for women. "I cannot believe Juliana is lost. I will never give up on her. Never."

"I understand, Sir Thomas, I do."

"Then, you know I cannot give up hope. Perchance the king keeps her hidden to keep her and the baby safe."

"You mean safe from me?" Ean shook his head. "She has no reason to fear me at this time and I do not make a habit of hurting children. I have listened for news of a child, but have not heard anything—not that I would be the first Merrick would tell."

"What about Hugh and William? They are still blessed by you. Can you find them? Are they here?" Thomas asked, feeling very alone. "Please, help me. I will do anything you demand in return."

Ean glanced around the tent, nodding his head. "Aye, Sir Thomas, I believe you would."

Hugh stormed out of the faery hall. How could that faery witch do this to him? And what was worse, he fell for it! He fell for her words, her seduction, her spell. Pushing past two men blocking the entryway, he strode into the courtyard. Fresh air assaulted him and he took a deep breath. It didn't help. Nothing helped. Walking out of the palace into the dimly lit forest, he suddenly stopped and frowned.

"Nicholas?" Hugh questioned, not turning to look and confirm what he thought to have seen. It couldn't be. Nicholas was dead. He'd seen him killed, burned into ash by King Lucien.

"Aye, Nicholas," William confirmed. "I found him in Lucien's prison. I could not leave him there to rot."

Hugh felt a mixture of excitement and regret fill him. The man, his childhood friend, was alive and yet he knew the full truth of what Nicholas had done. Juliana also knew, as she'd discovered the full extent of Nicholas' deeds, but William and Thomas were only told a part of the story. All knew Nicholas had killed Lord Eadward when possessed by demons, but they didn't know the full, slaughtering horror of the tale.

Nicholas had slain his father, stabbing him while he slept. Though the man had been possessed, Hugh feared him because there was a part of Nicholas who could've allowed it to happen—not to mention how Nicholas had knowingly covered the truth of it afterward. There was no way a man could do such a thing, possessed or not, and come away from it undamaged in some way.

Apprehensive, Hugh turned around to see Nicholas for himself, but was distracted from his purpose as he discovered the palace was gone, disappeared as if it was never there. He looked about in surprise as they stood surrounded by the forest trees.

For a moment, regret overwhelmed him as he realized Tania was gone and he might never see her again. He knew everything he'd felt for her was a lie, a spell, but he still felt it. The emotion, the happiness, the freedom from responsibility and worry had been real. He'd cared for her. She'd made him happy, for a brief time she had made him content. To have that, to taste the pleasure, to live in the bliss only to lose it as if it never existed, was a horrific feeling.

"Hugh?" William asked.

"Aye." Hugh forced all regret out of his mind, refusing to think of the faery queen. Nothing he felt for her could be real. The last year spent longing for her wasn't real. She'd done something to him to make his mind obsess over her and then she'd kidnapped him to finish what she'd started. Even now, the pull he felt had to be of her doing. Hugh hated her for that, hated her for giving him something false to cling to.

"Hugh?" William repeated. "Are you...?"

"I am well." The earl forced his attention from where the palace had been to his brother. Nicholas waited by William's side. The man's green eyes were dull and vacant. His hair was long, straggly, and he had a beard. Hugh had seen men who spent time in dungeons, had seen eyes in the faces whose spirits had been broken. Nicholas looked like such a person. "Are you sure it is safe to have him with us?"

"Who? Nicholas?" William glanced at the man. "He was in Lucien's dungeon."

"That does not answer my concern. The last I saw him, he was possessed by demons."

"Only one, I would assume," William corrected.

"Fine, possessed by a single demon."

"He looks all right to me." William had Nicholas by the arm and pulled him along as he walked, doing the same with an elfin male. "Aside from being confused."

"Who is that?" Hugh asked, looking at the elf.

"I know not. He was in the prison, as well as another just like him. I could only help these two escape, though I did try for the third." William led both dazed men forward. It was clear they couldn't move without assistance. "I am not sure what happened to them. They do not speak. Nicholas does not even know his name."

"Mayhap it is not Nicholas." Hugh eyed the man. It looked like Nicholas—a worn, beaten, tired Nicholas. "I saw Nicholas die. I saw him blaze up in flames. I saw his body turn to a smoldering pile of ash. A man cannot forget such things. This could be the demon that possessed him."

"And it could be Nicholas," William said. "Why would Lucien keep a demon chained?"

"To trick you and the woman with violet eyes, ah..."

"Mia," William supplied. "Her name is Mia."

"Mia probably freed you to make you think she was helping, when in reality, she was tricking you. It was by her hand that Lucien kidnapped me and brought me to Queen Tania. As far as I can ascertain, no one here is to be trusted." Hugh waved his hand to encompass the forest. "You were right all along, brother. Naught is as it seems in this world. The whole realm is a cursed, ugly, horrible place."

"Not all of it. Our realm is just as troubled. We humans have our own deceits, our own trickeries. Our kingdoms fight. Our—"

"I get the point." Hugh lifted his hand, cutting him off. "But in our world men use words and swords. Here they take away a man's will with spells and potions. How can we, as mortals, fight such weapons if our power to think, to feel as we should, is taken away? We are not equipped to live in the immortal realm."

"I never thought I would hear you say you were unequipped for any kind of struggle—be it a conflict or a war." William looked concerned.

"I will fight and deal with what I must, because I must. But I will not be so foolish as to ignore the very simple fact that we do not belong in this world. There is a reason the realms are separated. And, as soon as this is all over and we have Thomas and Juliana back in our fold, I'm going to dedicate my life to making sure Tania," Hugh paused, correcting himself, "to making sure none of this crosses over into Bellemare again."

"And the blessing?"

"I have faith that Bellemare can survive on the merits of its people," Hugh said. "We will make our own blessing. I do not want it if in so being blessed I risk losing my family."

"Do you know what you are saying?" William demanded. "If King Ean were to take his blessing away..."

"We are human." Hugh gave a small, unhappy laugh. "We build our lives on the merit of our birth, the goodness of our deeds. Bellemare can take its chances with the rest of the mortal realm. I am not afraid of hard work. I am not afraid to keep what is ours by my own merits. I will die for Bellemare if I have to."

"What did Queen Tania do to you?" William studied him. "I have never seen you this bitter."

Hugh had to turn away from his brother's probing gaze. He didn't want to think of Tania, of her deceit. "It does not matter."

"Faeries are different than we are, Hugh. They do not always understand the darker forces or that their actions can have darker consequences. Imagine if you will a nunnery—"

"I know you are not about to compare those loose moral faeries to holy nuns."

"They are not all of loose morals," William defended.

"From what I have seen, aye, they are." Hugh glanced around at the trees, trying to decide which way to go. Thinking of Tania's loose morals wasn't exactly what he wanted to be doing at the moment.

"This is beyond the point I am trying to make."

"Then what are you trying to say?" Hugh didn't want his brother to defend Tania or her kind. He wanted his life back, as it was.

"Faeries are beings of beauty and light. Their magic is rooted in it. To even see evil taints them and harms their magic. When I said they were like nuns, I did not mean they were celibate or God-worthy, I meant they are delicate, protected creatures. They live in their own world, like nuns in a nunnery, where the outside evil does not usually come. By nature, they are playful but innocent."

"You are going to have a very difficult time convincing me those women are innocents."

"Nay, not all of them are innocent to the ways of men, but they do not understand the miseries in life. They are not too familiar with the concept of death or violence. They do not face darkness or think of it. They—"

"I have no wish to hear this, William. Queen Tania is tainted. I could see well the change in her." He again looked around the forest, anywhere but at his brother's steady gaze. "That witch made a deal with Lucien to kidnap me. The Damned King almost killed me and he was going to kill you."

"It does not make sense," William said. "I heard you talking to Tania, Hugh, and I know you are angry with her. But Tania and Lucien? Together? It is not in her nature to make such an alliance. To do so would kill her and her subjects."

"Nothing here makes sense. All I have is what I know and I know Lucien brought me to Tania because she made a pact with him."

"Then she must really need you here to have made such a

deal."

Hugh couldn't believe that. Tania didn't need him. He was just an amusement. "If she needed me to come here, she could have sent an invitation. Nay, brother, methinks you think too highly of them. They are beautiful women and women tend to cloud your judgment."

"But—"

"Let us go." Motioning his hand that William should follow, Hugh walked away from where the palace had been. "We need to find Thomas. If I know our brother, he is here looking for us."

"Aye. Thomas would have found a way to cross into this realm. The only question is did he go to King Merrick or King Ean to start his search?"

"We will go to..." Hugh didn't want to say it. "We will go to Merrick first. Juliana is there. We might get lucky and find Thomas as well. If not, we will go to Ean from there."

"What makes you think our sister will come home with us? She chose Merrick. Do you really think she has changed her mind?"

"Because," Hugh looked at the dark trees, feeling as if their limbs somehow watched him. The leaves rustled, giving him chills. "We will not give her a choice."

# Chapter Eight

*Mystic Forest, Two days later...*

"I said, tell me the way to King Merrick's palace," Hugh growled, shaking the small creature before him. Green-brown eyes stared back at him, the color of mossy tree bark. They matched his long hair and beard, even his clothes. The gnome didn't answer so Hugh shook him again.

"He does not know," William said behind him. Hugh barely heard the words. "Let the gnome go, Hugh."

"Aye, let the gnome go," the gnome agreed, repeating William. "I do not know."

"Then tell me how to find King Ean," Hugh said.

"I cannot. There be a war," the gnome protested. "And I am not so sure you be good."

"Tell me!" Hugh yelled. The little man knew something. He had to. The creature was the first they'd come across in days.

"Hugh, please." William came to his side. He placed a hand on his arm. Looking at the gnome, he asked, "What is your name, good sir?"

The gnome gave Hugh a hard look, but the earl did not let go of him. "I be Dvorovoy Djedoesjka of the woodland gnomes at your service, kind wizard, but I be not at his."

Hugh snarled as the gnome nodded meaningfully at him.

"Do you know the way to either the Blessed or Unblessed King? And if not the direct way, the direction one must travel to get there?" William kept his voice soothing.

"Nay, kind wizard." Dvorovoy wrinkled his nose at Hugh. At the moment, the feeling was mutual and Hugh returned the look. "I cannot help you. The way is blocked to magic searchin'. The forest changes her mind, gives bad signs dependin' on what part of it you be in. You cannot even count on the moss to grow right and the dew beetles only run in circles."

"Is there any here that might know the way?" William asked.

"Afraid I cannot help you there. For directions you would be wantin' my brother, Domovoi. He is the found one. I am always lost."

"And where is Domovoi?" Hugh asked, his mouth tight. Was there a reason every creature in this realm needed to be difficult? If Dvorovoy hadn't tried to run away to begin with, Hugh would never have grabbed him. He looked at William. It has been two days since they left Feia and it wasn't lost on him what was to happen this day. It was the day King Lucien had planned to kill William—if Mia and Tania were to be believed. The knowledge made him harsher than usual.

"Tendin' his mud, I imagine," Dvorovoy answered.

"And where might his mud be?" Hugh was exasperated and it took all his willpower not to shake the poor creature until he passed out.

"I cannot tell you," the gnome said.

"And why not?" Hugh demanded.

"Because I am always lost," the gnome explained in exasperation, as if the answer should've been most clear. "Domovoi is the found one. He cannot get lost, I cannot get found. It be the way o' things. So how can I help you find his mud, if I cannot find his mud? Hmm?"

Hugh contemplated throwing the woodland gnome across the forest floor. It wouldn't help their situation, but he'd feel better.

"Hugh, let him go." William sounded very calm. "This behavior is not like you. You need to step back before you hurt him."

"Someone here has to know the way," Hugh grumbled. Anger was easier to feel than fear. His hold on Dvorovoy slipped and the gnome hurriedly grabbed his fallen hat from the ground and wobbled away, his short, fat arms pumping at his sides.

"Wait!" William chased after the gnome. The little man stopped, keeping an eye on Hugh. "If you were to try and get to the Unblessed King, which way would you go?"

Dvorovoy chewed on his lip, looking around. Slowly, he pointed the way Hugh and his traveling companions had come from. "I would try that way."

"Thank you, good sir," William said.

"Happy to help you, kind wizard," the gnome answered, before disappearing into the forest. Hugh looked, but could no longer see him as the gnome blended into the forest.

"What good was that?" Hugh asked.

"Well, if he is always lost, we know not to go the way he suggested," William said.

"Great, so that only leaves us a hundred other directions in which to go."

"I am only trying to help. I say we continue the opposite way Dvorovoy suggested," William nodded into the forest, "which is also the way we were going anyway."

"Forget the gnome." Hugh tried to think logically. "All right, so we have been walking for days. I know this has to be the right general direction. Juliana's sprights, Halton and Gorman, took us north from the faery palace to find King Ean, so now we head south."

"But the faery palace changes location within the forest," William put forth.

"I know that," Hugh said, his tone hard. He took a deep breath, trying to calm himself. Fear ate at him, making his temper shorter than usual. He hated feeling out of control.

While they walked, both Hugh and William had a chance to tell the other what had happened to them since leaving Bellemare. William thought Mia was really trying to help, but Hugh was hardly convinced his brother wasn't just enamored of the nymph.

Neither of them trusted Lucien or Tania for that matter. As more of his memories came back to him, which seemed to be more the further away from Tania's palace they went, Hugh recalled the Damned King with Juliana's dagger. That worried him. The last he'd seen the knife, his sister had it at Merrick's.

Hugh wished with every fiber in his being that he could be two men—one to save Thomas and one to rescue Juliana. How did a man decide which sibling to go after? How did he know which would need him more? Juliana had been in the unblessed palace for a year and it could be assumed Thomas was in the immortal realm for a short time. Which would need him more? Different scenarios played in his head, making it impossible to decide.

Forcing his tone to lighten, Hugh repeated, "I know that, William. But what else could I do? Ask Tania for directions before leaving? You heard her, she doesn't want me to leave this world. She threatened to kill me if I went back. And that accursed witch is why we are here in the first place."

William sighed instead of answering as he went to where

Nicholas and the elf stood waiting for him. The two appeared to be more lucid than when they first left the faery palace, but they didn't go anywhere or do anything without help or prompting.

"If we do not get to Merrick, we should find Ean." Hugh walked along the narrow path through the trees. In the distance, he heard a bird singing, but it was faint. Other than that, the woods were quiet. "At this point, I would settle for either king."

"I'd settle for ale," William muttered. "Or something to eat besides forest berries."

"B-ed," Nicholas said, his tone weak and stunted. It was the first whole word he'd uttered. He had made weak sounds and grunts but nothing coherent.

"Aye, that's right," William exclaimed, grinning as he slapped Nicholas on the back. "A nice, warm bed as well! Did you hear that, Hugh?"

The earl didn't answer as he turned to study their old friend. He didn't trust Nicholas, but he still felt affection for all they'd shared through childhood. The man was like a brother, not so close as blood, but nearly so.

"Bed," Nicholas repeated.

"Ah-ha! Aye, a bed!" William stopped in his progress to do a little dance.

"Wonderful," Hugh drawled. "Now they are going to start complaining for finer comforts."

"Blood," the elf whispered.

William opened his mouth, as if he would praise that man as well. He stopped, mid-motion and shook his head. "Did he say he wanted blood?"

"Aye." Hugh nodded, before drawling sarcastically, "Just

what this journey needed."

"Blo…" the elf tried again.

"You long for drink and this one—" Hugh began.

"Ah, nay, actually, I long for several draughts of ale," William inserted. "I long to be so drunk I am incapable of walking another step."

"Fine. You wish to be drunk, Nicholas wants a bed and that one," Hugh pointed at the elf, very suspicious of him, "wishes for blood. What manner of man did you rescue, William? Perchance he was in the Damned King's dungeon for a reason."

"Hmm." William studied the elf. "He does not look evil."

"Most evil men do not." Hugh frowned, thinking of Tania. His gut tightened. Nor do evil women.

Desire tried to fight its way inside him. Tania hardly looked evil. Nay, she looked more like a goddess. For a moment, he thought of her naked, her wings fluttering as they dropped little dots of light over them while making love. Even now he desired her. The only difference was now he could control the urge, could fight the lust she induced. His nose burned with the threat of tears, as if he would cry out, but he held the pain back, swallowing it down. He would not cry for her.

Responsibility had to come first. Before he was a man, he was an earl. The burden of it had never been as heavy as it was now. When he wasn't worrying about his siblings, he was worrying about his people and his horses.

"Cannot you do a spell?" Hugh turned in circles as he looked around. It seemed hopeless to continue on, but he knew he must decide a path.

"I already told you. I do not have my wand." William pulled Nicholas and the elf's arms and began walking toward what they believed to be the south. "The sky looks darker this way. It could be Merrick's palace."

"And it could just be nightfall again." Hugh sighed. William had made the same comment for the last couple of nights. He led the way over the forest floor, taking the two men with him.

"Aye," his brother agreed. "You never said, Hugh, what do you wish for?"

"Right now? A horse, a sword, my family and a spell to wipe away all knowledge of this place from our lives." Hugh snorted, adding to himself, *But, mostly, a way to forget the faery queen.*

Tania didn't move. She had no strength of will to. The silver walls around her were crumbling. Tarnished, broken chunks littered the floor like fallen stones. She wanted to find the will to carry on, but she hadn't the strength. Her magic was fading and she couldn't stop it. Her heart was tied to her magic, to all faery magic. And without her heart, she was dying.

"Roslyn," Tania whispered, not lifting her head.

"My queen?" The lady faery had been hovering nearby. Tania felt Roslyn lean close, but did not lift her eyes to look at the woman as she stared at a chunk of fallen ceiling.

"In the sacred chamber a scroll is hidden. Take your sister and find it. Without my purity, I can no longer rule. We must find another."

"Nay," Roslyn said, her voice frantic. "You do not know what you are saying, my queen."

"Aye, I do," Tania asserted weakly. "My reign is over. We must try and find a new queen."

"But, you have no child," Lily said. Tania should have

known both sisters were there. “Who will we give the crown to?”

“The queen does not need to be my blood,” the faery said. “We can find another.”

“Where are we going to find a pure faery?” Roslyn asked, her tone giving voice to the sheer impossibility of such a thing. Faeries thrived on pleasure and to find one who hadn’t partaken of flesh wasn’t likely.

“You must try,” Tania said. “We have no choice. I have failed as your queen.”

“Nay,” both said at once.

“You have ruled well,” Roslyn insisted.

“Very well,” Lily added. “We love you, my queen.”

“Do as I ask,” Tania ordered, finally finding the strength to look at them. “There is not much time.”

“But, Hugh...” Lily began.

“He might come back,” Roslyn added.

Tania wished she could be as positive, but she felt the truth inside her. She’d seen the anger in him. It wasn’t meant to be. Otherwise he would be by her side even now as her faery king.

“I am dying,” Tania said. Both of them gasped, their wings drooping as tears welled in their rounded eyes. “Go. Get the coronation scroll and find a new queen. Her blood and body must be pure and she must be willing to sacrifice. Call the others to help you. I do not know how much time I have left.”

The camp was quiet, as the morning was still new. Sunlight barely peeked through the trees and a soft, magenta glow surrounded the forest. Ean stood in meditative silence close to Commander Adal. They listened to the forest, enjoying the peace of such a moment.

Adal was newly appointed to the position, taking leadership right after the war had begun, but the commander was doing well in leading the army. He was skilled in combat. Though not the most seasoned warrior of the elfin army, he was smart and knew how to use his head. A leader had to be smart or men died.

"Word has reached us from High Leader Talan," Adal said. "He does not like that you send him to patrol the borders."

Talan had been passed over for supreme leadership when Ean named Adal the late Commander Gregor's successor. The high leader had no problem showing his displeasure over the decision.

"Leave him where he is," Ean said. "There is so much anger in him. I do not want him leading his men into battle and someone must watch the borders."

"But the western border? There is no threat from the ocean kingdoms. They do not care about the battles of land."

"Aye, but we cannot be too safe."

"He knows he is sent away," Adal insisted. "He knows you give the post only to keep him busy."

Ean knew Adal felt bad about taking the command away from Talan, but Ean had to go with instinct and his had told him to pick Adal. "There is little I can do about his feelings being hurt. Like I said, he is too angry to fight. Tell him to remain where he is."

"Aye." Adal nodded, again falling to silence.

Ean thought of the war, of his brother on the other side of it. He couldn't help but contemplate the thin thread that joined him to King Merrick. Blessed and unblessed, they were two very necessary sides to the same realm.

Thomas had been right when he spoke of the bond of family, but Ean was reluctant to admit he still cared for Merrick. The blood link of brothers was as strong as magic and it kept them connected to each other. The link between them had been calmer for some time. Queen Juliana could well be thanked for that. But, then, as the newness of his marriage wore thin, Merrick once more became disturbed. The Unblessed King always walked a thin line between blessed and damned. Ean knew King Lucien wished to take his brother. Even Merrick had begged him to sever the tie that bound them together. Ean couldn't bring himself to do it.

Why did his brother start this war? Why? Peace had been good. There was no reason to fight. The battles were pointless, the death they caused horrific. And yet, Ean and his men would fight because they must, because Merrick forced his hand.

"What is wrong with the trees?" Commander Adal drew the Blessed King's attention from within himself to the surrounding landscape. Ean followed the man's gaze up. Indeed, the color of the leaves seemed a bit pale and the wind did not stir them. "And, come to think on it, I have not seen any flowers for days."

"Or ferns," Ean nodded. Small plants normally covered the forest floor, but he'd noticed the earth looked barren. Dead leaves and broken limbs created a bed beneath the trees. "I see some moss, but not much."

"Should we be concerned? Does King Merrick try something?"

"This does not feel like Merrick. Flowers die in his presence, but do not stay dead." Ean closed his eyes, letting his magic pour from him, feeling the nature around him, sensing the wind and the trees. It was peaceful, but troubled. Frowning, he opened his eyes. "I felt..."

"Aye, my king? What?"

"I felt Lucien where the faeries should be."

"What does Lucien want with the faeries? Those meddling creatures are hardly ideal allies to a man such as him."

"True." Ean was glad Adal spoke without restraint. There needed to be open communication between a king and his commander.

"And I would hardly think Lucien seeks their company for a mere diversion. The queen would hardly stand for it. For faeries to take a demon to their bed would contradict their very natures and we have both heard the tales of Lucien's dark lust."

"I do not think it would be for lust," Ean answered, not liking this new sign. "Call a wizard—one of our allies. Have him cast a protection spell around the encampment."

"Do you think that is necessary? Anyone looking will sense the magic. That could lead Merrick right to us."

"Aye, I am afraid it might be very necessary. Merrick and his men might detect us, but I do not think they will come for us. They will think it a trap." Ean again tried to sense the faeries, only finding darkness. It was almost as if they'd been wiped out completely. Why would Lucien want to hurt the faeries? To take their magic from the land? And how exactly did he get close enough to Queen Tania to do whatever it was he'd done? "There is trouble in the faery world. If not for this war, I might have felt the shift sooner. The faeries have always been blessed, flighty, but blessed. They have never done us harm, but that does not mean they cannot be turned to darkness."

"Come to think on it," Adal mused, "there have been no faeries near the camp lately trying to seduce the men, or in the forest, working to mend broken leaves. Do you think Queen Tania has called them away?"

"Possibly." Ean cursed, kicking at the ground. "What would the Damned King want with the faeries? It does not make sense. Why faeries? Their magic is of no use to him in this world."

Suddenly, they both turned to look to where Thomas the mortal slept.

"But if not in this world," Adal began.

"Then in the mortal," Ean finished. "The scouts should be back very soon. If there is no immediate threat to the camp, I will ride with Sir Thomas to find his brothers. Mayhap the mortals will have some insight into this matter of the faeries."

"Doubtful."

"Aye, but it is all we have got at the moment. It's too much of a coincidence that the faery magic would darken around the same time the humans arrive. I will not take chances. I will not fight Lucien and Merrick both. If they were to join forces..." Ean shook his head, refusing to think about what would happen. "Balance is a delicate thing. In the past, the Unblessed Kings have been too prideful to fight with Lucien. Merrick is different. He was not born prideful, not like those that ruled before him. He struggles for balance. I feel it."

"What do the faeries have to do with Merrick?"

"All magic is tied. If Lucien cannot get Merrick, he might have formulated a plan to recruit the other races to his side. Such a force in the magical world would be hard to refuse. Lucien might make another try for Merrick's allegiance." Ean forced himself to appear calm, though inside he was perplexed. His men would look to him for strength and leadership. But who did a king go to for such things? Merrick had Juliana. Did she help to lessen his brother's burden? Loneliness curled inside him, but he fought it. There was no time for self-pity. "Or, Lucien's plan could be tied to the Bellemare family. Blessed souls have to be very tempting to a demon. Perchance Queen Tania has something to do with the mortals."

Adal made a small noise as he scratched his head. "When Lady Roslyn was in my bed, she told me the queen detained Hugh and Thomas last they were there. Methought little of it when she spoke the words, but it could be a connection between them."

"I will question Sir Thomas about their time at Feia with the faeries," Ean said. "Wake Raoul and Laurent and explain to them what is happening. They will come with me to find the mortals. And have them prepare my special mounts with extra for William and Hugh, should we come across them."

"Are you sure you wish to take the unicorns for this? With the Damned King's influence at Feia..." Adal paused. "Lucien would love to capture them."

"Aye, but I would have their magic with us. We have no idea what we are going to learn about Tania and Lucien." Ean took a deep breath and held it for a long moment, contemplating his actions. "I will wake Sir Thomas and see what he knows. Hopefully, all this will come to nothing."

"Blood."

Hugh frowned. It was all their elf companion would say, but he was saying it often. They traveled, theorizing that they'd eventually have to get somewhere. It wasn't as if they had a choice. They were lost after all.

"Blood," the elf said again.

"I am beginning to agree with you about this one," William said quietly from his side. Nicholas and the elf walked in front of them, finally able to move on their own. Hugh didn't trust them at his back. "He is a bit obsessed."

"Blood," the elf said again. He suddenly veered to the side, heading straight into the forest.

"Blessed saints," Hugh cursed. "Where is he going?"

Nicholas automatically moved to follow the elf.

"Ugh, grab Nicholas before he follows him," the earl ordered. William was closer and reached out to grab Nicholas' arm, stopping him. Hugh sighed heavily, trying to see where the elf went. "We do not have time for this."

"We could leave him," William suggested. "It would save us the aggravation."

"Nay, we are responsible for Sir Blood," Hugh said, reluctant. William saved the man, which made them honor bound to protect him if he was good or turn him in to face justice if he were bad. "I will go after him. He could not have gotten far. Wait here with Nicholas."

Hugh strode into the forest, listening for the elf. "Blood."

It took some searching before he heard the elf mumbling, "Blood, blood."

"Ho, Sir Blood." Hugh found the man sitting in a circle of sunlight.

The trees overhead were parted, giving access to the sun. The elf looked up before closing his eyes Wind stirred around them, as if calling to the man. A chill worked its way over Hugh's spine as he glanced around the quiet forest.

A low sound began in the back of the elf's throat. Hugh couldn't take his eyes off of him. He reached forward, trying to calm him. "Easy. What are you doing?"

The sound only grew. Suddenly, another cry rang over the forest. It was a hoarse, painful call coming from the direction of

William and Nicholas. The earl assumed it was Nicholas. The elf instantly began to scream as well, covering his ears as he fell to the ground. Hugh reached to where he normally carried his sword, but he had no weapon.

"What's happening?" Hugh demanded. The elf only screamed louder. Backing away, he didn't know how to help him. Turning, he ran for his brother, "William! William!"

Finally, Thomas thought, not for the first time since King Ean awoke him at dawn to look for his brothers. Waiting had been hard and he'd almost left the encampment several times. Only with no sense of direction, no weapons and no horse, it wasn't prudent for him to take off on his own. He understood that, being immortal, elves and such did not feel the need for urgency. To them, a day was nothing out of their eternities. To a human searching for his brothers, a day was everything.

The horse he rode was thinner than the Bellemare stallions, but it was a fine animal that turned nicely and was light on its feet. In every way the unicorn mounts looked like mortal realm horses with brown, black and white coats and large eyes. The only difference was they had horns protruding from the top of their foreheads, tipped with sharp, deadly points. Undoubtedly, the horn would make for very useful weapons in battle.

King Ean and two of his elfin guards escorted him through Mystic Forest. None of them said how they knew where to go and Thomas didn't think to ask. They'd given him back his sword and he reached to feel it as they rode, drawing comfort in its familiar weight.

Not saying a word, he followed the others' example and took the mount by its horn. He lightly nudged it to the side, directing it to turn. The beast nodded its head, following the direction, and they rode on in silence.

"Ahh!"

Thomas tensed. The scream came from the distance, loud and harsh. He'd heard such noises before—on the battlefield after a fight, when men lay dying in agony. "Who is that?"

"Sh," Ean waved his hand. "I sense Bellemare blood."

"What?" Thomas thought of his brothers, dying and bleeding in the forest. He kicked his stallion, holding it by the horn to direct it toward the sound. He had no weapon, no magic, but it didn't matter. His family was out there and he needed to save them.

"William!" Hugh yelled over the loud screams, looking for his brother as he pushed past the trees. "William!"

"Here," William called. He pointed, directing his attention at Nicholas on the ground several paces away from him. The man rolled back and forth, holding his head. "I do not know what happened. One second he's saying 'bed' the next he's screaming on the ground."

"It is the same with the other," Hugh answered, his heart wildly beating. He was glad to see William safe, but didn't let down his guard. "What's happening to them?"

"I know not." William pulled his robes closer. "Where is the elf?"

"Back in the forest. I did not want to touch him."

"You wanted to save me." It looked as if William gave a small laugh, but Hugh couldn't hear the sound.

"Nicholas!" Hugh leaned over him.

The man turned at the sound, his green eyes red and the skin around them swollen. He screamed louder, moving his hands to scratch at his eyes. "I did it! I did it!"

Hugh grabbed the man's wrists, wrestling them away from his face. Bloody trails were left over his cheeks where he'd clawed himself.

"William? Hugh? What is happening?"

Hugh turned, seeing Thomas swing off a strange horned horse. William answered, but Hugh couldn't figure out what he was saying. The youngest wasn't exactly the most helpful during physical skirmishes. Hugh tried to stand, but Nicholas thrashed and he was forced to hold on as the man flung his weight to the side, dragging Hugh to the ground next to him.

"Thomas," Hugh yelled. Thomas was instantly by his side. With his help, they pinned Nicholas, keeping him from hurting himself.

"I cannot tell you how happy I am to see you," Thomas said. "When that witch took you... Is this Nicholas?"

Nicholas managed to slip a leg free while Thomas was stunned with surprise. He jerked his knee, slamming it against Thomas.

"Ow," Thomas growled, locking his leg over Nicholas' to hold him still. Then, he put his hand over the man's mouth, pressing down to muffle his screams. "My ears cannot take this noise. What's wrong with him? How is he even here? Methought you said he was dead."

The thundering of horse hooves prevented Hugh from answering.

"Ow," Thomas drew his hand away. "He bit me."

Ean rode up followed by two others. He instantly lifted his hand toward them, saying, "Whoa, calm."

Nicholas jerked and went limp. Hugh pushed up from the ground. Thomas was slower to follow, shaking his hand. The sound of screams still penetrated from the forest where the elf lay. William hovered in the background, looking worried. Hugh wasn't surprised. William wasn't much of a fighter. He never had been.

"Thomas," Hugh instantly hugged him. "You are safe."

"Aye," Thomas returned the affection. "I was about to say the same to you. What happened?"

"Long story," Hugh said. Thomas went to William. The earl bowed to the king. "King Ean, I thank you for the safe return of my brother and for whatever you did to quiet Nicholas."

"You must tell me this long story, Lord Bellemare." Ean motioned him to stand.

"I would like to hear it as well," Thomas answered. "I was sure you were captured by Lucien."

"Aye, we were," William inserted. "But then Lucien gave Hugh to Tania and she tried to trap him to her, but he would not hear of—"

"William," Hugh interjected to get him to stop talking.

"Oh? Right, right," William said, sounding mildly distracted. "My apologies, my manners are..." He stopped to bow to King Ean. "It is an honor, King Ean, my brothers have told me of your blessing on Bellemare, well to speak truthfully, I knew of the blessing and told them of the blessing, but they told me of you confirming the blessing."

"William." Hugh gave a small shake of his head to get him to stop rambling.

"Ah, right," William said. "Pleasure, my king."

Ean started to speak, only to turn to look at the surrounding forest. "Who else is screaming?"

"I do not know." Hugh motioned toward where he'd left the elf. "William found Nicholas and an elf in King Lucien's dungeon. He rescued them."

Ean arched a brow and glanced at William, who was grinning profusely. "An elf you say? With Lucien?"

"Aye," William and Hugh said in unison.

"Let us see if we cannot quiet him so that we may speak." Ean began walking, his two guards right behind him.

"I would be careful, your majesty," Hugh warned. "He speaks of nothing but blood."

"Actually, he says nothing but the word 'blood'," William corrected.

"Right," Hugh agreed.

Ean didn't pause as he walked into the forest. Hugh turned to Thomas. "Tell me everything."

"Actually, brothers," Thomas glanced down at Nicholas, "methinks you'd better speak first."

Ean trudged through the forest, glad to have found Hugh and William safe. He'd sensed them, but it had been a faint call and he didn't want to tell Thomas they were close until he was sure. The man on the ground concerned him, as did the screaming man he now went to calm. Lucien's dungeons were a hideous place and it was hard to know what had been done to them while they were prisoners.

"My king, do you wish me to go first?" Laurent asked.

"Nay," he answered. "I feel no danger."

The cries became louder. Suddenly, Ean stopped, finding the man huddled on the ground. He lifted his hand to shower the poor elf with peaceful emotion when suddenly the man stopped yelling on his own. Dirty hands fell away from the man's head and slowly he rolled, turning so Ean could see his face.

The king froze, unable to move. The man's eyes met his, stroking a memory as distant as a dream but as real as his own hand. He couldn't breath, couldn't move.

"My blood," the man said softly, his hand shaking as he reached out toward Ean.

Ean stumbled forward, falling onto the ground next to him. He took the elf's chilled fingers. A tear came to his eye, as he whispered, "My brother."

# Chapter Nine

Lucien tapped his fingernails, deliberate and steady, against the arm of his throne. A great heat came from the center fire pit, illuminating the faces of the demons he'd summonsed to him. They filled his hall, awaiting his command.

Lucien let his eyes roam over them—so many hideous faces and even darker hearts. These were the pure breeds, demons spawned in pacts with evil, torn from their mother's thighs as soulless beasts. There was no hiding what these creatures were, not like half demons or the possessed who could appear like another race only to conceal the truth inside where none could see.

Nay, these demons were pure. Some had gnarled bodies, ravaged by time and hate. Others were like corpses, their rotting flesh peeled off their bones. Then there were the daimon, demons with flesh as red as blood and eyes as black as night. Those were to be truly feared. For the red daimon had the greatest power, the utmost hate, the largest appetite for destruction. They were unstoppable once they set to a course, so long as they had the means to fulfill it. Their only weakness was that they were trapped in the evil fires of his palace. They could not live in the immortal realm for long before being called back and, like Lucien, they could never travel to the mortal world—none of the pure demons could unless they attached themselves to the soul of a mortal. The daimon couldn't attach to a soul, for to touch a soul would be to kill it instantly.

"A new army will be raised," Lucien said. "A powerful army that will march across all lands raining death and destruction like a torrent from the skies."

"What kind of army?" a breathy, hairy lycanthrope asked, his fangs bared and dripping red.

"An army of half-breeds," Lucien said. "An army of your sons and daughters. An army created with your seed."

The statement got the excited reaction he expected it might.

"How might we do this?" a small, ghostly figure inquired.

Instead of answering, Lucien lifted his hand. He motioned leisurely to the floor, bringing forth a creature from the bowels of his dungeons—a tiny girl with long blonde hair and soulful blue eyes. When she smiled, the color of pale roses came to her cheeks. She was adorable, disgustingly so.

"Mmm, what a tasty treat," the hairy beast said, drooling.

"This will carry our seed?" A tall, thin ghoul snorted in disbelief.

"She is the soothsayer," one of his daimons snarled, putting out a hand to stop another from going forward to the child. The daimon bowed. "My lady."

The soothsayer giggled, the sound of happiness sending chills over the hall. Following the red demon's example, the other demons kneeled to the child, murmuring, "My lady," in respect.

"Tell them, Anja," Lucien ordered the child.

Anja smiled and curtseyed, gently lifting the skirt of her burgundy tunic gown. When she again stood, her eyes were filled with fire. Her voice rang innocently over the hall, happy and light, "I see a great ruler taking a dark throne. I see a great army of half-breeds marching through realms, conquering all races."

"What half-breeds? Elves?" a daimon asked.

"Half demon, half mortal," Anja answered. A series of grunts and whispers filled the hall.

"Mortals?" the ghoul asked. "How?"

"Magic." The soothsayer giggled. "Dark magic. Fire magic. Strong magic." She turned to Lucien, batting her now blue eyes. "And I see a dark prince."

Lucien froze. She hadn't told him that when they'd spoken before. The demons cheered. His gaze lifted up to the ceiling. Mia was in his bed, chained.

A prince?

"Now, let me go back down," Anja demanded, like the spoilt girl she was. She stamped her foot. "I want to play with the prisoners. Let me play."

Lucien motioned his hand, putting her back down into her playground in the lower dungeons. To his demons, he said, "You have heard the prophecy. I have brought you here for you are my most devious warriors. Contact your mortal priests and priestesses. The magic must be summonsed. Tell them to watch for the signs and tell your legions that any who father a half mortal child will rise in my favor. And, needless to say, I expect each of you to father a child of your own."

A couple temptresses in the corner huffed at the comment.

"Or mother them," Lucien amended. "My apologies, ladies."

"Seducing mortals is easy enough." A temptress bowed her head.

The group of women disappeared in a blink. Fire roared violently in the center pit, sucking the daimons in. A few ran for the door, others disappeared into a puff of smoke. He was left alone in his hall.

A dark prince. Anja saw a dark prince in his future. Lucien sat back on his throne, again tapping his nails in a slow and steady rhythm. Now that he was alone, he called the soothsayer back to him.

Anja appeared, her arms crossed over her thin chest and her lips in a pout. "I knew you would call me again."

"What do I have to do?" Lucien narrowed his eyes on her.

"You are doing it," Anja said, giggling. "Queen Tania. She is weak and she cannot find another to take her place. If you finish her, the faeries will join you or die. The faery rings will be left and they can call the mortals through. They will fall unsuspectingly into our world."

"You said a dark prince," Lucien clarified, though Anja's words about Queen Tania were enlightening. He would pay her a visit just as soon as he was done with Anja.

The soothsayer laughed as she swayed back and forth, lifting one hand into the air and then the other as she danced. Lucien let music fill the hall. So long as she was happy, Anja would help him.

"You are doing what you need to do," she said. "All will happen in time."

Tania felt as if the floor spun beneath her in slow circles. Faces drifted by like a dream, but still she didn't move. Her hands lay above her head and her legs sprawled out over the floor, stiff and straight. She stayed in the main hall, unable to find the energy to leave it.

Faeries came and went, sprinkling flower petals around her

like she was already dead. She let them, hoping with each new visitor a worthy successor to her throne would appear. Tania told herself that is why she waited, why she held on to each breath.

One never came.

"My queen," Lily whispered. "We found the old spell. It will tell us who should take the throne."

Even though it was what she had to do, she still felt a pang of sorrow at the thought of ending her rule. This is not what she wanted. Worse was her sorrow over losing Hugh. She loved him, desperately, and she wanted him back. But just because that is what she wanted, didn't mean that it would happen. Hugh had to want it too and it was clear he didn't. Not once did he say he wanted her. Well, once, but he'd been under the euphoria of her pheromones.

"Should I cast it?" Lily asked.

Tania moved her eyes, unable to speak.

"All right, my queen, I will cast it. I will do it," Lily said, nervously. "Roslyn, come, please."

Roslyn instantly appeared.

"Here, read this," Lily thrust the piece of parchment at her.

"I...?" Roslyn hesitated, before reciting the ancient words to cast the spell by herself. Lily backed away, not helping her sister.

Tania watched Roslyn's lips, not really hearing what she said. Suddenly a soft glow illuminated the parchment. Roslyn dropped it. The light moved, settling over Tania. She felt the tingling of faery power on her, but was unable to control it. Slowly the glow concentrated on her hips and disappeared.

"There is no one else," Lily whispered. "The magic picked you, my queen. There is no one to take your place."

"We are lost," Roslyn said, stumbling back. "Lost. Queen Tania, what will we do?"

"The magic has nowhere else to go," Lily continued. "What will happen to us, my queen? Please, what will happen to us? The magic will be lost."

Tania wanted to scream with frustration. They were right. The magic was in her. She was the last faery queen.

"What will we do?" Lily's cry echoed over the hall. Tania wasn't sure if Lily was screaming at her or the other faeries. A low murmur of panic swept over her court. She couldn't lift a finger to stop it.

"What will we do?" Lily repeated, falling down to rest next to the queen on the floor. Roslyn lay behind her sister, her cheek pressing against Lily's so both faery ladies were staring at her. "Tell us what to do."

"We need you," Roslyn whispered. Tears welled within their troubled gazes. "If you do not tell us what to do, who will? We need a queen."

Tania closed her eyes, unable to look at their pleading faces. She had never realized how dependent they really were on her and her magic. How ironic that the one time she took something for herself was the one time she was failing them. Was it wrong to want happiness? To want Hugh? Why couldn't she have one thing for herself?

A cold chill swept over her and she felt the flower petals blowing. When she opened her eyes, it was to a dark, shadowed hall. Lily and Roslyn were no longer next to her.

"Such changes." Lucien's voice sounded moments before he appeared to stand above her. His feet were on either side of her hips as he leaned over to study her face. "You look beautiful."

Tania couldn't answer. It was no wonder the others had left. None of them would want to brave Lucien's presence.

"Ah, poor faery. You do not want to die, do you?"

Tania looked to the side, not seeing any of her faeries, before staring back up into his black eyes. She felt abandoned. Lucien gracefully kneeled over her, straddling her waist with his knees. The chill continued up her body until she shivered uncontrollably.

"Little faery, what did Lord Bellemare do to you?" The Damned King caressed her cheek before moving his hand to rest over her heart. Gasping, he closed his eyes and took several stunted breaths before pulling it away. When he again looked at her, his gaze burned and he was smiling. "Ah, your pain." He leaned over her, rubbing his cheek next to hers, breathing hard as if aroused. "Such sweet heartbreak." A tear slid from her eye and he licked the trail, following it with the tip of his tongue. "Such delicious sorrow." His tongue veered off-course and ran over the part of her lips. All of a sudden, he kissed her hard, stealing her breath before letting go. "Your pain makes me want you, but you are broken. Used. He used you, Tania, did he not? Lord Bellemare used you and now he is gone, leaving you to die."

More tears slid from her eyes.

"Look how he has left you, poor little faery," Lucien continued. "Look at what he has done."

Fire blazed on the tips of his uplifted fingers before forming into a silver mirror. He held it over her. Tania didn't want to see, but she couldn't stop herself from looking. Her hair was black, as were her eyes and lips, even her tears. They contrasted what pale skin she had left. The dark lines had grown over her, a vine attesting to her sorrow. No wonder the faeries cringed away from her. She didn't recognize herself.

"Give yourself to me. Give me your soul and I will give you peace," Lucien promised. "You know I have that power. I can free you. I can save your faeries if you pledge yourself to me."

She shook her head in denial. The slight gesture was enough. His face contorted in irritation.

"He has done this and you still love him?" Lucien growled. "He used you, Tania, used you and left you. I promise never to leave you."

She knew he was lying and regretted the day she'd made her pact with him to bring Hugh to her. Time would have shown Hugh back to her if that is what fate wanted for her. She should have never pushed. But she defied fate and was selfish. This dark punishment was her reward for such greed.

That was all done with. She had a choice to make. Did she save herself and faery magic by agreeing to serve the Damned King, or did she take the consequences of her actions? If she saved the faeries, what would she be saving them for?

"As you wish, my queen," Lucien said when she did not agree to his terms. He stood and threw the mirror, which puffed into smoke before hitting the ground. "I kept my bargain and now it is time for you to keep yours before you die. I get my night in the mortal realm."

"Step..." Lily tried to say, her voice weak. Tania couldn't see her, or her sister.

"Step back," Roslyn added.

"Stay away from her," said Lily. "Get out of here. She will never agree to your offer. Leave this palace at once!"

Lucien tossed back his head and laughed. "As you wish, little faery."

Tania moaned as Lucien wrapped them in darkness, knowing he carried her away from the palace, away from her subjects and friends. They had made a blood pact, a foolish bargain which she would be forced to keep. Perhaps that is why she had yet to die. She had a deal to uphold. The balance of all magic demanded it.

"Merrick." Ladon didn't say much, but he did say his brother's name. Often.

"What did Lucien do to you?" Ean asked, not for the first time. Nearly sixty years had passed since he had seen Ladon, but it didn't matter. He knew him the second their eyes met. His brother was alive.

Ladon looked worn, but being imprisoned for as long as he had been would do that to a man. When he spoke, his voice was hoarse from little use, but he did speak and, though the words were sparse, Ean could understand what he was trying to say.

"Merrick," Ladon repeated. Ean had told him of Merrick's new kingdom, but had gotten little of Ladon's story from him. It was clear his brother didn't remember all that had happened to him, or much about where he'd been for the last sixty years. All Ladon knew for sure was that he urgently wanted to see Merrick. Ean didn't know why. All these years he thought it Merrick's fault Ladon and Wolfe had died. Now, Ladon was here and Wolfe was possibly kept prisoner in Lucien's hold.

"Merrick is not the same brother you remember," Ean tried to explain. "After you disappeared, he took the unblessed throne. He started the war we now fight. There is no blessing on him, not anymore. I fear what he will do to you. Your powers are weak, Ladon, I feel that they are, and you do not remember everything that has happened to you. Merrick might take advantage of that and turn you to the unblessed. I do not know what he is capable of anymore. I want to believe the best in him, but I cannot."

"Merrick," Ladon insisted, his eyes hardening with determination. Ean had forgotten how stubborn he was when he wanted something.

"How can I deny you?" Ean answered, not wanting to let his brother leave but unable to think of a good excuse to make him stay. Every reason he had was a selfish one. "The Bellemare brothers ride to see their sister, Juliana. She is Merrick's wife. You may go with them. But I will be listening for your call, Ladon. If you need me..." Ean took a deep breath, desperately not wanting to let him go. "Please, reach out to me if you need me. When you are done at Merrick's, come back so that I may protect you. I'll bring you home and summons the best magical healers in the realm to help you. You will be safe at Tegwen."

"Yesterday." Ladon glanced at the earl, Thomas and William who waited beside some of Tegwen's horses with Nicholas. Ean had sent the unicorns back with Laurent only to have the elf guard bring back regular mounts so Merrick wouldn't get his hands on the unicorns. He'd been right in his instinct to initially bring them on this journey. The unicorn's power was what had most likely guided him to find Ladon.

"I know it was like yesterday to you, but it has been fifty-seven years since you disappeared." Ean wanted to ask him again what had happened, but Ladon didn't know. Mayhap seeing Merrick would help him remember. Then, there was the small part of him that believed Merrick had a right to know Ladon lived. And Wolfe, who could even now be alive and imprisoned.

Ean couldn't think of a way to get into Lucien's prisons, but Merrick might be able to. If Wolfe was alive, mayhap Merrick could find him. Ean hated feeling helpless, but in this situation he was. It was very possible Merrick could do more.

"Take care and come home, Ladon," Ean said, knowing he had to let him go. "Just come home."

Ladon nodded, lifted his hand, hesitated and then patted Ean's arm. It was the first willing sign of affection he'd given. Ean covered the hand briefly before letting go. Ladon turned to join Hugh and the others, swinging up onto a horse that waited beside Nicholas'. The Blessed King watched but Ladon didn't look back as the group rode off into the forest.

Hugh didn't care that Nicholas wanted to go home or that Prince Ladon wanted to see his brother. How could he after what Thomas told him about his visit to the Black Palace to see their sister. Merrick was hiding Juliana from them and he had no way of knowing if she was safe.

Worry flooded him with every beat of his heart—worry for his family, worry for Bellemare and the horses, but surprisingly also worry for Tania as well. He couldn't get the faery out of his head and he kept seeing her face as he'd left her on her palace floor. There had been something in her eyes, something he hadn't wanted to see at the time. And her voice, how it had pleaded with him! Just to remember the tone cut him to the core. She sounded as if she'd been heartbroken. Even if that was true, there was no reason for him to worry about her. No one died of a broken heart, not really.

Despite his best efforts, Hugh realized he loved her. He loved the faery queen. But how did he know if that love was real? What if it was only a spell? How could he ever know for sure? If he felt love for her, and that love felt real, then did it matter if it was of his doing or not? And why was he even allowing himself to think about it? Nothing would come of him and the faery queen. She belonged here and he belonged at Bellemare. They came from different worlds.

A pain came over him as he thought of her.

*No one dies of a broken heart*, he assured himself.

"It would be better if it was a spell," Hugh said thoughtfully. He rode faster, wanting the journey to be over. *Then it will not hurt once I get her to take the accursed thing off me.*

"It was." William matched the earl's new pace, catching up to him.

"What?" Hugh blinked, coming out of his thoughts. He hadn't really been paying attention to the fact that others could be listening as he mumbled to himself. It only proved how preoccupied he was.

"What happened to you at Feia? It was euphoria," William said. "That is what you were talking about, is it not? You had that look on your face. The look you get when you think of Queen Tania."

"I..."

"You do get that look." Thomas joined them, riding along the opposite side William was on. "What is euphoria?"

"That is what the faeries call the little bits of magic that wrap you in pleasure and suspend the mind from all rational thoughts." William sighed heavily. "You experienced it, Thomas, when Tania trapped you in her palace and the faery ladies came to your bed to give you pleasures upon pleasures upon plea—"

"Mmm," Thomas nodded, grinning. "I like euphoria."

"They drug you and take away your will," Hugh reminded his brothers. "No pleasure gained is worth that cost."

"Faeries cannot help it, not always."

Hugh frowned, seeing matching expressions on his

brothers before they all turned around to look at Prince Ladon. Nicholas rode beside him, staring off into the forest. The man didn't say much, but Hugh didn't expect him to.

"The euphoria," Ladon said, his tone flat. "When faeries are excited, they put off pheromones—the little magical lights you see coming from their wings. It happens when they are aroused, or during sex, or for some even if they are in love or feeling great overwhelming bursts of pleasure. Their magic overflows out of them because it is so powerful that they cannot contain it. If you do not fight the magic, the feeling will consume whoever it touches—thus the reason it is called euphoria."

"You are talking," William said, stunned.

"I do not know why I remember that so clearly when everything else is a blur." Ladon ignored William's declaration of surprise.

"Who doesn't want to remember faery euphoria?" Thomas chuckled before catching Hugh's eyes. His smile faded and he cleared his throat.

"Perchance you are right. I found much pleasure in the arms of faery ladies. I can remember pleasant things," Ladon mused.

"So you suffered this euphoria?" Hugh asked.

"Nay, not fully. It is too unpredictable and one can never be sure when the spell of it will end. Elves know how to protect themselves against falling into the feeling completely." Ladon was staring at Hugh when the earl turned around to study the elf's face. "But for those who do not, it can be all consuming."

"That is my point," Hugh said. "Drugged. She knew what she was doing."

"Who?" Ladon nudged his horse closer. They rode into a clearing and all four horses fit side by side. Nicholas didn't join them as he stayed behind.

"Hugh?" Thomas asked, when no one answered.

"Queen Tania," Hugh said through gritted teeth. "She drugged me with this euphoria."

"Mmm, not possible," Ladon dismissed, shaking his head. "Unless... Has a faery king been crowned?"

"Nay," William said.

"Then it cannot be the queen who did it to you," Ladon said. "It is not possible. Are you sure it was not one of her ladies? They enjoy games."

"Why would you say it cannot be Queen Tania?" Hugh frowned. He'd been there. He knew very well what Tania was capable of and he definitely knew who she was.

"She is not like the others," Ladon said.

"You mean she does not have the pheromone?" Thomas asked.

"I am sure she does," Ladon answered.

"She does," Hugh confirmed.

"But she would never use it," Ladon said. "Not for sex. Not in such a great amount as to hold a man under her spell. She cannot."

"Ah, right, right," William pointed at him, getting excited as he squirmed in his seat. "Wait, but she did. So that means..."

"Right what?" Hugh demanded. "Means what?"

"You know." William gave him a meaningful look.

"Know what?" Hugh reined his horse to a stop. "William, out with it! I have no patience for this conversation or your mysterious ramblings."

"You know, Hugh. That Queen Tania is, was a virgin before you and she..." William touched the earl's arm. "You did realize she was untouched, did you not? I do not see how you could miss such a thing as that."

A maiden? Hugh wasn't sure what to say. It couldn't be true.

"Hugh? How could you not know something like that? I realize it has been a long time since you have been with a woman, but..."

"Why did you not tell me?" Hugh directed his question more at Tania who couldn't possibly hear him or answer.

"I did not think you would miss such a thing," William answered. "Truly, Hugh, if you would like help with the fairer sex, I would be happy to give you some instruction as to how to—"

"Nay," Hugh said hastily, nudging his horse in the side to get him to move along the path, away from his brothers and Prince Ladon. He did not want to talk about his time in Tania's palace anymore. "Sixty years ago when you knew her Prince Ladon, she might have been innocent, but there is nothing innocent about the woman who took me to her bed. She knew what she was doing."

Even as he said it, he wasn't sure. Their first time together had been a blur. Hugh nudged the animal again, causing it to dart in front of the others. Within moments, the sound of horses' hooves was behind him, beating against the hard earthen path.

"Hugh!" Thomas yelled.

Hugh, not wanting to slow, leaned low against the horse's neck and rode faster. Forget saving the horse's legs by taking it easy. He needed to get to Merrick's castle.

"Hugh, hold! It is Nicholas! He is gone," yelled William. "We cannot leave him behind."

"Blessed saints!" Hugh sat up, looking behind him.

Whipping his horse around, he galloped back down the path. As he passed his brothers, he ordered, "Try to find him."

Hugh slowed, studying the ground for signs that a horse veered off course. The ground was uneven and the path worn. It was hard to tell. Not knowing what strange urge unexpectedly compelled him, he jumped off the mount and walked straight into the woods without any clue as to where he was going.

All around him, the forest became dense—too dense to see through to any distance. Leaves fell around him like gentle yellow-gold raindrops, covering the floor and crunching under his feet as he walked. It was early in the season, too early for falling leaves, but Hugh stopped trying to make sense of the immortal realm. Little spots of light danced along the floor, shining through the high tree limbs.

Then a voice carried over to him, stopping him as it said, "I beg you, take it away..."

# Chapter Ten

"I beg you to take it."

Hugh frowned. Nicholas was speaking, imploring actually. His voice sounded clear, nothing like he'd expect from the lethargic man he'd been escorting around the forest.

"I do not want to live. Please, take away my pain. I'll give you anything you want, just make it stop. I do not want to see anymore."

Who was Nicholas talking to?

"You know the price, Sir Nicholas," a familiar voice answered. Hugh could never forget the smooth nature of that tone. It was King Lucien.

Hugh stopped as the leaves turned black and fell upon varying shades of gray earth. Even Hugh's skin was gray, as if something sucked the color from his flesh, from his clothes and from the forest. Behind him, he saw light and color, but where he walked, where Lucien and Nicholas were, there was none.

Good sense would bid him to turn around and go to his brothers, to run away from this madness, but honor compelled him forward. How could he abandon his friend, no matter his sins? He was not Nicholas' judge.

Hugh stepped around a tree. Nicholas knelt on the ground, his arms wide and pleading as he beseeched King Lucien, "Aye, take my soul, end my pain, take my soul."

"Nicholas, nay!" Hugh shouted. "You do not know what you ask for."

"I accept." Lucien's head was lowered as he looked down at Nicholas. He lifted his eyes to Hugh, filled with fire and hate.

Nicholas shook violently and was slower to look at him. Tears poured from his eyes and he sobbed, "Leave this, Hugh. This does not concern you. Leave it."

Lucien kicked Nicholas in the chest, sending him flying backward with a hard grunt. Nicholas hit the ground and skidded along the forest floor. He kept weeping.

"I have been waiting for you, Lord Bellemare," Lucien said. "I knew you would come for me."

"I came to find Nicholas so that I could bring him home," Hugh said. "He is not himself."

"Of course he is," Lucien waved at the fallen man. "He is exactly himself—a pathetic mongrel. See how easily his soul is broken and bartered? He gives it to me, just hands it over. Most people who come to me are desperate to trade for something they think has value. But, Nicholas, he just comes to end his own pitiable suffering."

"Let him go. What do you want with a broken soul?" Hugh asked. He made a move to go to Nicholas.

Lucien lifted his finger to stop him. "How much do you love him, my lord? Would you trade me your soul for his broken one?"

Hugh opened his mouth to speak. A great part of him wanted to say "aye", but a deeper part of him whispered that Nicholas was not worthy of saving. Nicholas made his choice—he killed Lord Eadward and then lied about it.

"Hugh..." Nicholas stared at him, crying, pleading. Hugh

didn't know what he pleaded for. Did he want saving? Did he want death? All Hugh knew for sure was that Nicholas had become a broken man.

"Ah, come on, Hugh? Where is my valiant knight, ready to save his family and friends at any cost to himself? He is like a brother to you, is he not? You grew up with him, trained beside him, fought with him. His only crime was falling in love with your sister and wanting to be a part of the precious Bellemare family." Lucien chuckled. "Can you really let him give his soul to me, when you know I would have something far greater from you?"

Hugh opened his mouth, staring at his childhood friend, torn by their past and what he knew of the present. The words wouldn't come.

"The demon killed Lord Eadward," Lucien continued, "not Nicholas. Are you going to let him suffer? Where is your honor, Lord Bellemare? He is your friend!"

Hugh still could not answer. He didn't trust Lucien to tell him the truth. For all he knew, Nicholas wasn't Nicholas but a demon—just like in the memories of the past Lucien had shown him. This was exactly why he hated this realm. Nothing was as it seemed.

"So be it," Lucien said, when Hugh didn't answer. Nicholas pushed up from the ground, trying to stand.

Time appeared to stop. Leaves froze within the air and the faint sound of the wind through the trees turned silent. Nicholas collapsed on the ground, falling helplessly onto his back as he stared up at the trees. His sobbing ceased as he just lay there. Hugh had seen broken men and Nicholas had no will left to live. With one word, Hugh could stop Lucien, but at a great price. He swore that he'd find a way to free Nicholas' soul, but not at the cost of his own.

Lucien held out his hand, lifting it toward Nicholas. Fire came from his fingertips, deep red flames that wound through the air like smoke, curling a path to the fallen man's face. The color was strange against the gray hue of Lucien's colorless world. Hugh closed his eyes, trying not to look. But he found himself opening them to watch as the fire circled a petrified Nicholas' face.

Nicholas gasped as Lucien's power entered into his nose and eyes. His back arched and he convulsed. Hugh wanted to go to him, tried to, but his feet did not move.

"Cease," the earl whispered, but Lucien only smiled.

And then it was done. Lucien drew the flames back toward him, letting them enter his eyes and nose as they had Nicholas. He jerked, gasping in what could only be called extreme pleasure. Nicholas lay on the ground, unmoving. The man hadn't even screamed, but Hugh could see that what happened hurt him.

"You were right about him," Lucien said when he could again speak. "His soul was hardly worth the time it took to extract it. I am actually glad you did not trade for him. It would have been too disappointing for me to watch you fall for this unworthy one."

"He was not unworthy." Hugh stared at Nicholas' face and slack jaw. Perhaps now the man had some peace in death. "He was lost."

"Arrrh!" Nicholas suddenly shot up, breathing heavily as he stood on his toes. With each harsh breath, an audible rasp resounded over the quiet forest. His voice a hiss, he said, "My king."

"You did not think he was dead did you?" Lucien asked, as if reading Hugh's shocked expression. "The soul is gone, but the man lives on. No pain. No worries. No remorse or regret. Just base, primitive man in all his soulless glory."

Nicholas looked at Hugh, his eyes hard dark pits. The earl felt a cold chill at the sounds he made.

"Go," Lucien ordered. Nicholas was instantly sucked into the ground, disappearing from sight.

"I will repay you for this," Hugh said.

"He asked for this, Lord Bellemare. I only gave him what he wanted—an end to the pain inside of him. How can you fault me for that?"

"He did not know what he was doing," Hugh argued. "And it is your fault he was lost to begin with. You made him murder his father."

"He knew well enough." Lucien threaded his hands behind his back. "I gave him the demon that provided him with the strength to murder his father. I did not make him do anything he did not desire to do in his darkest fantasies. It was his words that called to me, begging anyone who could hear him to help end his pain, to make Juliana his. I answered his call when no one else would. If he did not truly want what I gave him, he should have taken more care with his words."

"I am not listening to your lies, demon."

"However will you live with this?" Lucien ignored Hugh's angry outburst.

Hugh said nothing.

"So you would not trade for Nicholas," Lucien continued, "but what would you trade for?"

"You have nothing I want."

"That may very well be, my lord, but let me show you what I have before you naysay my offer." He held out his hand. Hugh refused to take it. "She is waiting for you to come and save her."

Juliana? Hugh stiffened. Who else could he mean? He

searched the Damned King's face, but knew he couldn't trust him. What else could he do, though? If there was a chance this monster had Juliana and would do to her what he'd done to Nicholas, he had to stop it. His sister was a good person, an innocent—Queen of the Unblessed or not. Nothing would ever convince Hugh otherwise.

Reaching forward, he took the king's hand. Fire burned him as they erupted into flames and he felt himself being sucked through blackness. Before long, he was dropped on the great hall floor of Lucien's palace. Orange firelight erupted over the dark stone, giving light to the entire place.

"Where is she?" Hugh demanded. "Where is Juliana?"

"Juliana?" Lucien laughed. "I did not say Juliana."

"Then who?"

Lucien pointed to the fire pit. Hugh quickly circled it, hoping the king didn't mean inside the flames. Then he saw Tania, her small body on the floor, motionless. Everything about her had changed, but Hugh knew instantly who she was.

"Tania?" he whispered. Without thought, he ran to her. This is not what he'd wanted for her when he left. Lifting her shoulders, he pulled her head into his lap as he kneeled on the floor. Inside, he yelled in fury and fear as she didn't respond. "What did you do to her, Lucien? What did you do?"

"So you do care for her," Lucien said. "I had wondered on that detail. Though one thing troubles me, how can a man such as you leave a woman he cares for to die?"

"I did not leave her to die," Hugh said, pulling her into his arms. Her mouth was close to his neck and he felt her weak breath on his flesh. "I left her to find my family and bring them home." He shook his head in disbelief, feeling along Tania's side for injuries. "Why do you do this? She is your ally!"

"My ally?" Lucien chuckled, loud and cruel. "The queen has

never been my ally, Lord Bellemare."

"But...?"

"Our dealing?" Lucien leisurely strolled, as if time had no meaning. "She made her pact with me out of desperation. There was no way for her to bring you here on her own."

"Desperation?" Hugh stroked her soft cheek, willing her to look at him, to give a sign that she would live. Severe pain seized hold of his heart and squeezed it tight. He didn't want her dead, never dead. Sure, he'd been angry with her at what she'd done, but he didn't want this. He wanted her alive, so that he may always picture her in his mind. If fate wouldn't allow him to have her, then he would have the dream of her to carry with him.

"Love and duty will do that to a creature," Lucien whispered. "Because of you she is dying. At first, I admit I was surprised by her desire for me to bring you here. The faery magic had been depleted for some time, allowing my demons into your precious home, and I never really understood what had caused the shift. And then I saw her face as you lay dying on her floor the day I brought you to her.

"She loves you and it is that unrequited love that is killing her. Tania knew this and did the only thing she could—she brought you here to love her. But you didn't love her, did you? Nay, I'll wager you resented her for having me kidnap you. But, before you left her to her fate, you took something from her, didn't you? You took her innocence, the sacrifice she must make to rule her people and keep the faery magic. In taking her maidenhead you struck the final blow to her heart. It is you who is killing the faery queen, Lord Bellemare, not I. My interest in her is so she may complete her end of the blood pact that brought you here. That is why she is at my palace."

Hugh hugged her closer, rocking her in his arms. "Tania,

wake up. Look at me."

She didn't move.

"Faeries are creatures born of light. They do not fall in love easily, but once they do it is forever. Look at her, Hugh. Such a fragile creature cannot survive heartbreak. What she did, she did to save her people, but also to save Bellemare from me. There is no other to take her place, for a virgin faery is a rare creature indeed and because of you there is no such thing anymore." Lucien held his hands to the side and laughed. "Do you not see what is happening? When Tania dies, her magic will die, taking all faeries with her unless they pledge themselves to me. Whatever faery magic remains will be under my control and my demons will march freely over the realms. Your precious Bellemare will fall. And, without faeries to tend the land, there will be no one to help nature, to grow, to plant, to tuck seedlings in at winter so that they may again spring to life. People will starve and in their desperation they will pledge allegiance to me or die."

"Nay." Hugh would not let Lucien win.

"What do you propose, Earl? Sir Nicholas' soul was not enough to persuade you, but what about Tania's life, the life of Bellemare, of your realm?" Lucien sped forward with unholy speed to grab Hugh by the face. "I told you that we would not always be enemies. I told you one day you would come to me, beg to join me. This is your chance to make things right by Tania. Give yourself to me to save her. You love her, I can feel it, even as I can feel you do not want to love her. I can take away the confusion and fear. I can give you pleasure. After, if you still want her, I will give her to you. She will be your bride, at your side on the new throne of Bellemare where you will lead my armies over the mortal realm."

"And my family?" Hugh shook.

"Safe," Lucien promised. He patted Hugh's hair, stroking it. "And right where you would have them—at home, at Bellemare with you. I can give you the power to protect them. You cannot protect them now, can you? Juliana is lost and you nearly lost your brothers. It is so hard keeping them safe, but it does not have to be. I offer you, I offer them, an eternity of life. You never have to worry about their safety again—so long as you all pledge to me."

"I..." Hugh looked down at Tania, unable to think what to say. He was scared for her and didn't want to see Lucien sucking the soul from her as he did Nicholas. His heart would never recover from such a loss. Aye, he'd been angry with her, but only because he loved her and the thought of her betrayal had hurt.

He loved her.

Hugh hadn't wanted to admit it because the admission only brought pain and fear. They were from different realms with duties and responsibilities. What they had could never be and by admitting he loved her, he had to face the fear of never having her. But, each time he told himself how different they were, how useless it was to love her, the less it seemed to matter.

"It is so easy," Lucien whispered, tempting him to give in. "Just say 'aye'."

Hugh ignored Lucien, as he leaned over to kiss Tania's lips. Keeping his mouth close, he whispered, "Come back to me, my love. Do not let the darkness have you. Do not let Lucien win. I never meant to hurt you. If I had understood, if I had known, I would not have left you like this. You must forgive me, my love, I do not know this world of yours. I do not understand it, but I know now that I love you. I've loved you since the first. We'll find a way to be together, even as I must remain at Bellemare and you at Feia. We will find a way to make it work. Ladies in the mortal realm see their husbands off to battle, separated for years and they all find a way to make it work. We can work this out, Tania, but first you must awaken."

"What are you doing?" Lucien demanded. "Do you really think saying the words now will help your cause?"

"I love you, Tania, come back to me. Please," Hugh said.

Lucien growled, storming around him with a look of desperation. "You can never go back to Bellemare! Even if she does hear you, she made sure of that when she sent me. Ask me of the blood pact. Ask me what I get out of it. I'll tell you! She is going to allow me into the mortal realm so long as I brought you here and did not harm your family for a fortnight, not forever but a mere fortnight. That is who you claim to love."

"First you'd have me believe her a saint that I should trade my soul for and now she is unworthy?" Hugh asked logically. "Which is it Lucien? Or do you even know in all your manipulations?"

"If you go back to Bellemare without joining me, you will die," Lucien said. "She sent me not only to get you, but to make sure you could never leave. You were bitten by the walking dead in the stables, were you not? If you leave this world, you will become like the corpse you fought—dead and possessed."

"That is why you told me I'd die if I went back to Bellemare," Hugh said softly to Tania. "You were trying to warn me."

"Warn you?" Lucien kneeled in front of them, lifting his hands as if he would touch Hugh, only to pull back. "She did it."

"You control the demons," Hugh said, in a moment of vivid clarity. He wasn't sure how, but he felt as if a warm heat came over him where he held Tania. "I do not believe you, Lucien. I see your deceits for what they are. I have dealt with mortal men like you. Deceit is deceit, no matter the realm. I see that now."

Lucien made a weak, angry noise. Hugh looked down. His hands had a soft glow where he held her, matching the glow on her body. As the glow spread, the darkness on her disappeared. The black vines turned to a white, wintry blue and the black ran off her hair like water, trailing toward Lucien's knees as he stayed kneeling before them on the floor.

Tania quivered in his arms, her lashes fluttering as she looked at him. Her dark clothing changed to a beautiful gown of soft material. It shimmered in the firelight, like sunlight on fresh snow sparkling like diamonds. The bodice was tight, hugging down to her hips and flaring into a flowing skirt adorned with tiny roses.

"Hugh," she whispered, gazing up at him. She looked so beautiful, so healthy yet she felt fragile in his arms. He wanted to protect her, to hold her close and make sure no one ever hurt her.

"Keep doing whatever it is you are doing," Hugh told her. His body tingled, itching along the spine and around his head.

"I love you," she said, breathless. The queen smiled at him. It was a weak look, but made his heart soar. "I feel you. I felt you calling me. I heard you. I love you."

"I love you," Hugh said. "I am sorry for everything."

"Argh!" Lucien yelled. "Stop talking!"

Hugh held Tania tighter.

"I am sorry you cannot leave." She fisted her hands in his tunic. "I did not mean for it. I did not mean—"

"I know." Hugh cut her off.

"I still get my night in the mortal realm," Lucien demanded. He stayed away from their glowing bodies as if the magic of it kept him back. "You made a blood pact with me, Tania. You have to honor it. I upheld my end. I brought Lord Bellemare here. I left his family unharmed for a fortnight."

Hugh, with the aide of Tania's power, had knowledge flowing inside him. He instantly understood. "Nay, William."

"I took him before the pact," Lucien said.

"But he hurt himself in your prisons," Hugh said.

"What?" Tania asked, confused.

"William complains about the ache in his body constantly," Hugh explained. "That is enough of a harm, is it not?"

Tania nodded. "Aye, it is."

"Nay!" Lucien screamed. He lifted his hand, calling a rush of fire to him. "What are a few bruises?"

"Lucien!" Before the Damned King could call the flames to him, Mia darted out from behind a column. She dove for Lucien's waist, knocking him to the side. "Let them be. You lost. Let them be!"

Hugh stood, pulling Tania up with him as the two fell. Tania's wings started to flap, as she said, "We should go."

Hugh began to walk.

"Think of yourself as small and use your wings," Tania ordered. "We need to fly out of here."

"My wings..." Hugh reached behind his back only to feel the silken texture of wings protruding from his spine. He walked in circles, trying to see them. "My wings?"

Hugh felt faint. Why did he have wings? And why could he feel them flapping in response to his fear as he was lifted off the ground.

Tania wasn't sure how it had happened, but she wasn't

about to stop and question her good fortune as she led the way from Lucien's castle. As Lucien kept her in darkness, she'd heard every word they said to each other. Hugh knew the truth now, but she could feel that he forgave her and understood. And, for her, she felt his love for his family, for Bellemare. She had always understood that he cared for them, but now she felt his emotions as deeply as he did. A small fear welled inside her to know the sorrow he would feel once he had time to really contemplate never returning to the mortal realm, but she would find a way to help him protect Bellemare. Her happiness depended upon his. They were intertwined, two halves to a whole.

Hugh loved her. He said he loved her and she knew it was true because she was alive. And with those sweet words, he'd saved her life and faery magic. He was her king and he finally sprouted the wings to prove his rightful place at her side. Only he didn't know how to use them yet.

Hugh flew in a circle, gradually moving closer and closer to one of the hall columns. Tania grabbed his arm inches from impact, jerking him higher, out of harm's way. Below them Lucien screamed and she heard his slave arguing with him. Tania could do nothing for the woman. If she were to save her, Mia would only be returned to Lucien when he wanted her back.

Tania felt heat approaching and pushed Hugh out of the line of Lucien's fire. Flames shot past them. He kicked in the air and she imagined he was having a hard time controlling his new wings.

"Hugh, look at me." Tania took both of his hands in hers, sending her power through him to help him transform to a miniature size. He did, poofing into smaller form. "Now, do not think, just fly."

✧

"I do not like this." Thomas tethered Hugh's horse to his. He looked around the forest where they'd found the mount. None of them could detect any sign that the earl had gone into the trees, only the fact that he wasn't there.

Nicholas' mount had been hiding in the forest and appeared after their calls. William and Thomas searched in the direction it came from, but found nothing.

"We cannot leave without Hugh." Thomas looked at William.

"Merrick," Ladon said.

"Do not start that again," William answered, "though it is better than 'blood'. What was that about anyway?"

"Ean and Merrick are my blood," Ladon explained.

"Ah," William said, nodding. "Methought you meant blood-blood, not family blood."

"Morbid," Ladon said.

"Aye," William agreed.

"Was Merrick here?" Thomas interrupted. "Do you sense him?"

"Nay, but I must see him," Ladon said.

"I am not going anywhere without my brother," Thomas said.

"He is not here," the elf assured him. "He is gone. We had best be gone too. There is nothing we can do here."

"I am not leaving without him." Thomas didn't care if Ladon was a blessed prince. He wasn't about to leave Hugh behind. "So if you want to see Merrick, you had better help us find

Hugh."

"What about your sister?" Ladon tried to appear calm, but Thomas saw his eyes darting to the side in apprehension. "Merrick can help you find both of them. We need to go."

"He could be right," William said. "We looked through the forest. There is no sign. Most likely they were pulled through a portal of some sort."

"Fine," Thomas grumbled. "But this is one game I am tired of playing."

Tania led Hugh from the Fire Palace into the forest. She flew as fast as she could, careful not to dart too quickly around passing tree limbs. Hugh was still too new to his wings to control where he flew.

"I want to go by ground," Hugh said, sounding weak.

She glanced back. His face was pale and his eyes were rolling in his head. He looked as if he was about to be sick. Tania slowed her pace, leading him to perch on a branch.

"What has happened to me?" He flapped on his wings hard, wincing slightly as he was pulled back by them. She darted forward to keep him from falling over the side. "I feel different, light. Everything is so large."

Tania followed his gaze up. She was used to changing her size, but could see how the gigantic forest might be unsettling to him. A bird swooped to land on the branch behind him. The animal was the same size as they were. Hugh jerked around to face it, reaching for his waist as if he'd find a sword.

"Shoo." Tania motioned to the bird. The creature again took to flight.

"What is happening?" he asked again.

"You have turned." She was afraid he wouldn't be happy with the change. "My love has turned you. I promise you will get used to them."

"Is there a way to get rid of them? I cannot let my brothers see me like this." Hugh reached behind him, turning on the branch. Then, as if noticing his wobbly position for the first time, he looked over the side and stiffened. He grabbed his stomach. "I would much rather be on the ground. Man is not meant to be so high in the air."

"Hugh, I am sorry." She reached for him. His eyes met hers. "But, I promise to find a way to get you back to Bellemare. I know you have to go and find your family. I know you have to get them safely back to Bellemare. And do not worry about the wings. I'll help you cast a glamour over yourself. No one will see them."

"Tania," he tried to break in, his voice strained.

"I understand now," she tried to say everything she wanted to, "but you cannot go with them. I am sorry. You will die if you go back there. I cannot heal you of the affliction Lucien's demon cast upon you. I am so..."

Tania sobbed, unable to continue.

"Tania—" Hugh grabbed her by the arms and pulled her forward to his chest. She clung to him and the trees stirred.

"But Merrick might have a way." She wondered why she hadn't thought of it before. She felt better than she had since meeting Hugh and her head was clear. "Aye, Merrick. I am sure he will be able to do something. The forest whispers that he has a very powerful witch in his dungeons. She can bring the dead back to life. If anyone can do something—"

"Tania," Hugh tried again.

"I know, you have to go find them," she cut him off. "I will send you to the Black Palace, to Juliana. I am sorry for all of this, for hurting you, but I did it because I love you."

"Tania," he said louder. "I love you, too. I do not blame you and I am sorry for not understanding why you did what you did. I do now. I love you."

"Oh." She made a weak noise of pleasure.

Hugh opened his mouth as if to continue speaking, but instead drew her forward into a deep kiss. She melted into his arms, her knees weakening. Suddenly, Hugh jerked back with a gasp. She opened her eyes only to realize they'd fallen off the high limb and were wildly plummeting through the air. Tania quickly righted them, helping him to the ground.

The forest wind picked up and she listened to the trees. "The forest is telling me you must go. Now. Lucien may follow us and your family needs you."

"I am sorry for leaving you," he said. "I am sorry I did not take you gently your first time in my bed. I did not know you were—"

"You do not have to say it. You saved me and my people." A tear slid over her cheek. She didn't want to let him go, but he didn't belong here. He loved Bellemare too much and there was nothing she could give him to compare to that. "Let me now do the same for you. Come, there is a faery ring over here. It will take you to the Black Palace."

"There is so much we still need to say."

"I do not feel like we have time." Tania led him to a small ring of dark grass on the ground. "I need to get back to my palace. My faeries need me and your family needs you."

"You are right. I have to save them." His eyes didn't leave her as he searched her face. "I have to make sure they are unharmed. William and Thomas were left in the forest and

Merrick refused to let Thomas see Juliana. Then there are the horses—"

"Mmm, nay, worry not about the last foal. I will send my ladies to watch over it. They will assure it is safe, if it has not been born already."

"I have been thinking. If we take some of the elfin stock with us, I am sure I can still save the line. It might take a few generations, but we will get it back."

"You have to go, my love." Tania tilted her head, gazing up at him, her eyes glowing with all the longing in her heart. "I understand you have to go back. Bellemare, the horses, your people, they need you."

"Duty always beckons." He touched her cheek. "And we as leaders must submit to its will."

"It would seem there is never time for us, is there?" Tania gave a small, sad laugh.

"I am sorry, but—"

"You are right, you have been right. I understand that now, Hugh. I did not think about it before. I never realized how much my faeries depend upon me until I watched them fall apart as I lay dying. They could not find any to take my place. I am all the faeries have. Without me the magic dies." Tania had grown used to their neediness, so much so she didn't realize how much they'd been draining her, how lonely she'd been. No wonder she'd been drawn to Hugh. He didn't need her, never had. "Honor and duty demands we do what we must, but the sacrifice seems too great this time. Regardless the loss, we are both forced, are we not? But if you could decide, if Bellemare did not need you, would you choose to stay with me?"

"Aye," he answered without hesitation. "I would. I will. I will come back for you, Tania, I promise. This time I will come back."

She gave a short laugh. “I have been told that before.”

“I’ll be back,” Hugh swore, pulling her to his mouth. He kissed her deeply, as if he’d never let her go. She wanted to live in that moment, the moment when the purity of their love was so strong it raced in her blood and beat his name in her heart.

*Hugh. Hugh. Hugh...*

Tania shivered, looking up as he broke the kiss. She wanted to believe him, but she knew this time she could forgive him if he didn’t make it back to her. She pulled a stray hair off his tunic and wrapped it around her finger to keep it so that she may watch him from the sacred pool. “The trees urge you to hurry. It grows colder. Lucien leaves his palace.” She glanced at her skirt, grabbed the hem and tore a small piece of material off. Then, grabbing her wing, she shook magic off it into the cloth. Tania made a satchel and handed it to Hugh. “Shake this and think of growing to your normal height. It will help you.” Then, saying a few ancient words, she motioned her hand over him. His wings disappeared. “That will keep your wings from view and use until someone takes the glamour off.”

Hugh reached behind him. “I cannot feel them.”

“They are there,” she assured him. “Just hidden.”

Tania leaned toward the small faery ring, pressed her hand in the middle of the magical circle and hummed softly as she thought of Merrick’s palace. A soft white mist came out of the ring like fog. The queen stood and faced Hugh, lightly kissing him. She wanted to hold him forever, but there was more to the world than just the two of them.

“Find your family,” she told him, firmly pushing him into the middle of the ring. The fog swallowed him, taking him to the Black Palace. “See them safe.”

# Chapter Eleven

Hugh didn't want to leave Tania, but he had no choice. He promised himself that when his family was safe, he'd go to her and figure out what was between them. Love for her flowed through him, ending the torment he'd felt in his soul, squelching the anger he'd carried since meeting her, easing the frustration. But with the love came another fear—a fear he'd been carrying but was now magnified until it gripped his heart.

Whatever had happened in Lucien's hall had connected him, made him understand her, as clearly as his own thoughts. She never meant to hurt him.

As he came out of the fog, he clutched the satchel Tania gave him to his chest. Though the blue of moonlight, he looked around, unable to see past giant stone walls that ran along both of his sides, trapping him in a narrow valley. Beneath him, two lighter gray lines faded into the darker stone. They arched away from him, as if forming a circle whose sides were hidden beneath the stone walls.

Hugh tucked the satchel into his tunic shirt. Slowly, he climbed up one jagged cliff, using the narrow outcropping of rocks for footing. The hard rock scraped his hands as he pulled himself up. His flesh stung, but he didn't care. He'd get a better view from the top. It took some time, but he finally made it, pulling himself over the edge onto solid ground.

Out of the corner of his eye, he detected a moving column. Only after looking intently at it, did he realize it was a blade of grass swaying back and forth in the gentle breeze, silhouetted by the light of the moon. He was still small in stature, a fact that continued to make him uneasy. Hugh was not a small man by nature, but now he felt like a field mouse lying in wait for the falcon to swoop down.

Without wings—wings he didn't really know how to use anyway—he couldn't easily move over the clumps of earth that formed a wide path of churned dirt. Trees towered over him like impossibly high castles.

Taking the satchel, he did what Tania instructed. As soon as the dust of her magic sprinkled his flesh, the sound of her laughter washed over him. He caught the smell of her on the breeze and closed his eyes, aching to hold her, really hold her. He could feel the gentle brush of her body in the wind.

Hugh didn't want the sensation to end, but as it lightened, he was forced to open his eyes. The world was as it should be, of normal proportions. He was right where Tania said he would be. The ominous lines of the Unblessed King's palace stood like a blight against the darkened sky. Along the top, spires twisted and curled like a knotted limb reaching for the heavens. He was finally there.

Lucien's soul burned with rage. Hugh and Tania? How? He'd been so careful, waiting for the perfect moment to act, watching as all his plans unfolded.

He had taken Sir Nicholas' soul so the earl could see, so he would know the true power of the Damned King. Next, he watched as Hugh went to Queen Tania. When he saw how the mortal did care for the faery queen, he made sure to reveal the true cause of Tania's darkening nature, knowing the earl would feel guilt. Lucien never imagined the earl's love would be strong enough to bring her back, but had bet on guilt making Hugh trade him for her life and soul. If that didn't work, he'd let her die and he would have the faeries' powers on his side to help him cross over whenever he wanted and to bring the mortals to him so that his demon army could be born. Eventually, Hugh would have crumbled and made a pact to go back home—once the demons invaded Bellemare and threatened all he loved.

"At least without me, he can never go back to his precious home." Lucien had underestimated Lord Bellemare once again. He was strong and honorable. It made the Damned King want him more.

Lucien snarled, slowly letting his gaze travel up the large fire in the center pit of his hall to where Mia levitated, ready to be dropped into the flames. The stone columns had stretched out to hold her, wrapping her legs and trapping her arms to her chest. Another band went over her mouth, keeping her from talking as it pressed tight against her. All it would take was one small direction of his power and she'd be dead.

He couldn't do it.

Summonsing a small blue demon, he threw fire at the creature as soon as it appeared, killing it. He didn't feel better. Mia's feet kicked, but she couldn't get loose. Anger burned inside him at her deceit. How dare she help Lord Bellemare! How dare she keep betraying him!

Lucien willed the stone to bring her to him as he stood from the throne. It moved silently through the air, growing as it drew her forward. He was dressed, one of the rare times he allowed himself to be clothed. The long, red jacket covered his naked chest, held together with cross-lacing down the front, only to swing open around his legs. The red breeches were low on the hip and tight.

When Mia was held before him, her face level with his, her body parallel to the floor, he grabbed her jaw and pried her head back so she was forced to look at him. He stared into her wide, violet eyes, soaking in her betrayal.

"You conflict me, Mia." He didn't let the stone band off her mouth. He didn't want to hear her voice, not now. "I give you everything and you continually betray me. I know it was you that freed William and Ladon, and now you help Lord Bellemare and Queen Tania escape."

Her eyes widened at the admission.

"I told you, Mia, I know everything you do. I knew as you gave yourself to me, scraping my flesh and drinking of my blood." The demon was burning in his eyes and he didn't even try to stop it from taking over him. Lucien hoped the demonic rage would kill her, for he could not. The more she betrayed him, the more he wanted her. It was her defiance that made his blood quicken.

"And it is her treachery that will be your undoing," a small voice said behind him. "You must take better control of her. She will destroy you if you let her continue without restriction."

Lucien didn't need to look to know Anja was there. He must have unwittingly summonsed her to him.

"Is the chance to create an army lost?" He stared at Mia.

"The loss of the faery magic is unfortunate. Your greed for Lord Bellemare has set back our plan," Anja said.

"Do not lecture me, soothsayer," Lucien ordered. The fortune teller giggled innocently, a sound that sent chills over him.

"As you wish, my king." Anja skipped around the floor, going beneath Lucien's prone captive, only to climb up a curve in the stone that held Mia in place. She walked along, her arms out to the side to keep balance as she made her way toward the ceiling. As she neared the column feeding the stone path, she turned, sat and then slid back down to the floor.

"Anja, quit playing games," Lucien ordered.

"Huh." She pouted, sticking out her lip as she jumped down off the stone. "Then let me go back down to the prisons and make me an arc like this one. You never give me gifts anymore."

"I give you plenty, soothsayer."

"What about her?" Anja pointed at Mia. "Can I have her? I promise not to kill her. She cannot die, not yet."

Lucien considered it. Anja's eyes looked greedily at Mia.

"Aye," he said. "Mayhap some time in your care will teach her to behave."

Mia tried to scream, but the sound was weak. She thrashed about. Lucien kissed her forehead, whispering, "You brought this on yourself, sweet nymph."

The stone pulled her, yanking her back into the column. It sucked her into its depth, swallowing her into the bowels of his palace. Anja disappeared with a giggle. Lucien lifted his chin and strode from the hall. Tonight he would sleep alone.

"It would appear this is a time for family," Merrick said, sounding slightly amused. They were in his hall. Thomas, William and Ladon had beaten Hugh to the palace. Merrick had sensed Ladon and had snatched them from the path to bring them to his home—horses and all. There wasn't much time to discuss it, but Thomas did manage to whisper that Merrick had been at a loss for words as he looked at Ladon. In turn, Hugh had told him quickly of where he had been.

"Here is your magic back." Thomas set a packet on the table. "I did not need it."

"Keep it," Merrick said, glancing at Ladon. "You never know what the future may hold. After I send you back to Bellemare, you might have a use for it."

Hugh didn't even want to know what they were talking about.

"You look changed." Merrick eyed Hugh. "Are those wi—?"

"Aye," Hugh said quickly, knowing by Merrick's expression he must have seen through the glamour over his new wings. He reached behind his back, unable to feel them. Since his brothers didn't react, he could only assume they couldn't see them. Merrick chuckled, still looking very amused.

Hugh gave a meaningful glance at Ladon, who sat quietly at the long banquet table that graced the great hall. The table curved from Merrick, who was at the seat of honor. Thomas and William were on one side, Merrick's brother was on the other. A chair appeared by Ladon, as if welcoming him to sit. Hugh moved his gaze to Merrick's. "I want to see my sister."

Merrick didn't move, save for his eyes going to the side where Ladon was. Hugh knew the king understood his meaning. He had brought him Ladon, it was only right that Merrick show him Juliana.

"What has happened to her?" Hugh asked. "I know King Lucien has her knife, the knife we gave her, the knife she had last we were here."

Merrick looked surprised by the news. "Lucien? Are you sure?"

"Aye," Hugh nodded.

"It was probably stolen by one of the goblins and lost. They are constantly causing mischief. I will punish whoever it was." Merrick said. "I would have felt another's magic in this palace. Lucien was not here."

"So she is here," Hugh concluded. "Why do not you call her to greet us?"

"I cannot. It is as I told Thomas. She is in the garden," Merrick said. "She will not be coming out any time soon."

"Take me there." Hugh stood, fists on hips.

Merrick looked at him for a long time. "She will not leave with you."

"Methinks that is her decision," Hugh insisted. "Will you keep her here if she wants to go home with me?"

Merrick gave a small laugh. "If she tells you she wants to go home with you, I will not stop her."

The Unblessed King stood from the table. Thomas and William made a move to follow him. Merrick held up his hand. "I will only take one of you. I cannot guarantee all of you will pass through the garden maze unharmed."

"But," William began in protest.

"We have a right," Thomas said at the same time.

Merrick looked at Hugh, not answering them.

"I will go," Hugh said. Merrick nodded. Thomas and William continued to protest. Ladon didn't move.

Merrick led the way from the hall, taking him through a door near the throne. A small round window with the silhouetted head of a dragon was on top of another door. Merrick opened it and paused. "Stay directly behind me on the path. Stray and you will fall into eternity."

The moon was bright, looming over the enclosed side yard.

A dark wall encased the area, making it impossible to see out. Merrick stepped down a black cobblestone path. Grass was on either side and it led to an arched entryway into the gardens.

"Where is the fall?" Hugh asked.

Merrick kicked a stone on the edge of the path. It disappeared into the cut grass, as if falling through. "There."

As they went under the entryway, the vine-covered walls of the garden soundlessly parted. The red flowers eerily looked like they were covered in blood.

"Stay close and do not touch the vines," Merrick ordered. "They will slice through you like a blade."

When Hugh looked back, he saw the path was closing them in as they walked. It wasn't long before they were in the center section of the garden. The area was enclosed by vines, the ground covered in stone. Hugh had no doubt Merrick was keeping his sister prisoner. He looked around for her, but all he saw were benches, statues and empty vases.

"Where is my sister?" Hugh asked.

"William saved my brother," Merrick said. "I had no choice but to bring you here. It is what Juliana would want."

"Where is she?"

Merrick motioned to the stone statue on a platform in the center. Hugh looked at it for the first time, stunned to see his sister's face frozen in the stone.

"I do not understand." Hugh slowly stepped forward. "You had this carved of her?"

"You asked to see her. This is your sister, trapped in stone."

"Enough of this," Hugh demanded. "I want to talk to my sister."

"Then speak, but she is not saying much these days,"

Merrick answered, his voice rising by small degrees. Hugh saw him reach out as if to touch her outstretched hand and then drew it back. "And before you start yelling any louder, she did this to herself. I have come here every day trying to find a way to get her out."

"To herself?" Hugh did not believe it. "Juliana turned herself into stone?"

"Aye. I would have sensed another's magic in my home. I found her like this and brought her out here so she would be safe. There is nothing I can do. I have tried everything. All I can do is wait for a sign, even if it takes thousands of years."

"You did this to her," Hugh whispered. "Mayhap not directly, but if she'd have been with me at Bellemare, she would not be like this."

"About that," Merrick said, "you have the smell of the undead about you. I do not think you can go back to Bellemare."

"Why even warn me?" Hugh said, more to himself.

"It is what she would want." Merrick studied his wife.

"It is because of you she is like this."

"I smell faery on you, as well." Merrick gave him a meaningful look. "Am I wrong, King Hugh?"

"King...?" Hugh hadn't taken time to think of it. He reached for his back, not feeling the wings.

"Methought as much when I saw the wings beneath the faery glamour. Tania made you her king. It is just as well. You cannot go back to Bellemare. If you do, you will die."

"I was told you might help me to go back." Hugh loved Bellemare and didn't want to leave it, but he loved Tania even more. He longed to have both.

"And why might I help you?"

Hugh took a long look at his sister. Juliana's features didn't move. He silently urged her to speak to him, to give a sign. She didn't. "Because it is what she would want you to do."

Merrick gave a slight smile and laughed. "Aye, it is what she would want, is it not?"

Tania watched the panels floating above the divining pool. They all showed the same thing—the way back to Bellemare from the Black Palace.

Her palace was back to normal. The faeries were celebrating in the above hall, dancing and drinking and sneaking off into the hidden parts of the palace to make love. They had much reason, as their lives were just as they were before—joyous and blessed, light and good, happy and free.

Tania was happy for them, but she couldn't be happy for herself. Hugh loved her. In that all her dreams had come true. Nothing else would ever compare to the knowledge. She loved him with her whole soul. But, Hugh was honor, duty and responsibility. Hugh was Bellemare. If Merrick could save him, would he go back to his beloved home?

It seemed an eternity, waiting in the sacred chamber, watching the panels for the travelers to pass by. She knew with a strange certainty that they would leave King Merrick's for Bellemare. Her powers had come back to her with a vengeance, almost as if they were stronger from being so dormant the last year as she pined for Hugh.

She saw Thomas and William first, walking as they led their horses toward the portal to Bellemare. Holding her breath, she waited. And then there he was, with his brothers, leading his horse forward like the others. The image of him turned around and she saw the proud lines of his face. Tania shivered, slowly nodding in acceptance. It wasn't surprising. Hugh was going back to Bellemare, back where he belonged.

"May all the magic of the faeries be with you, my king, until fate brings us together again." She blew a kiss to him.

She waited as they swung up onto their horses and rode for the now visible front gate of Bellemare castle. Only when they disappeared inside, did the panels fall back into the divining pool.

Her wings fluttered, lifting her off the stone island. She had a celebration to oversee. Duty was all she had, duty and the dream that one day Hugh would be free to come back to her.

Thomas led the way up into the great hall, followed by a crowd of excited servants and knights welcoming them back. It was all he could do to smile as the men greeted William and a healthy Hugh behind him.

"It looks as if you were ready to celebrate." Thomas looked around at the tables. Food was being set out, already prepared.

"Aye. In the circumstances, methought it a good idea. The last foal was born this morning." Geoffrey had been in charge of the castle while they were gone. Turning to Hugh, he announced, "Healthy and perfect."

Hugh gave a slight smile and nodded. Thomas hid his frown at the less than enthusiastic gesture. Sweeping forward to grab Hugh's arm, he excused, "He is still tired. Come on, brother, let us get you to bed. I will have a maid bring you something to eat."

Geoffrey nodded in understanding and they took their leave. William didn't follow as he was already leaning against the head table speaking to a pretty servant.

"You have so much to learn." Thomas led the way to Hugh's room. "And I have so much to teach you. The Bellemare horses are the pride of your people. This birth is the most joyous news the castle could receive. You will have to be more excited about it in the future, but not too excited as you are very serious of nature."

"Aye," Hugh's voice answered him, dejected. Thomas stopped, taking a deep breath. It was still eerie, hearing the sound coming from the man. He looked like Hugh, talked like him, but only he and William knew it wasn't their brother.

Turning, he started to put his hand on his arm, only to pull it back. "Ladon, I know you are lost, but I need you to try."

"I will," he promised.

"Thank you," Thomas said. "I know this cannot be easy."

Ladon nodded. "I could not stay there. I needed time away, so thank you. Please, show me where I may rest and you go celebrate your horses. Tomorrow we will start my training."

Thomas nodded, leading the rest of the way to Hugh's chambers. "A maid will bring you food. It will probably be best if you send her away. My brother's been celibate for nearly a year."

Hugh grinned as he saw his wife walking into the hall. Her head was held high. The gesture bespoke of her regal bearing. She was truly a fine queen. His queen.

He was sure he'd never seen anything quite so lovely in all

his life. Her toes pointed toward the ground as she floated through the air. The silk of her gown hugged her lithe body and the long skirt trailed behind her on the floor. His eyes devoured the way the white material clung to her breasts and hips, shadowing and lightening with each movement. He became entranced. The sound of music faded into the background of his mind and no one spoke. They hadn't since he'd walked into the castle without help.

Being king of the faeries obviously came with some strangely innate abilities—finding his new home was one of them. The Silver Palace called to him, as Tania called to him, with the promise of joy and happiness. It was hard to leave Bellemare, but the same power that led him to Tania and his new home also told him that his people were safe for now.

It was hard to give up his title, but in his heart he'd always be the earl and no matter where he lived, he'd love and care for his people. Besides, it wasn't Tania's fault King Lucien had ordered a walking dead man to attack and kill him. Merrick could do nothing for him, or wouldn't. Hugh wasn't sure. He didn't trust the man. At least he'd be closer to Juliana in this realm. Out of all his family, she needed him the most. He swore to find a way to help her out of her stone prison.

"You are stunning." Hugh did not care that the entire hall could hear him. Let the faeries know he loved the queen. When he looked at Tania, he saw his future and he was happy. Duty and responsibility never looked so bright. Together they would take care of her faeries and his people.

Tania blinked several times and her wings stopped as her feet dropped onto the hall floor in shock. Her lips parted as she gasped and she glanced over her shoulder the way she'd come only to look back at him. "But...?"

"I told you I would come back for you," Hugh said.

"Aye, but..." She smiled happily, running for him. Her wings flapped, causing her to lift up slightly so she was on her toes. Hugh opened his arms and she jumped into them, crashing into his chest. Around them faeries cheered.

Hugh held her tight, meeting the soft press of her mouth as she kissed him. Tania's tongue delved inside. She tasted sweet, like berries from the forest. Her hands gripped his tunic as if she would pull it off him.

Hugh chuckled, leaning back. He felt as eager as she, but the sounds of the hall suddenly penetrated his brain to remind him they were not alone. "Why do not we go abovestairs, my queen?"

"Aye, my king." Tania moaned, pulling him with her as she backed toward the stairwell that would take them to their chambers.

"Wait?" Lady Lily rushed forward. She held out a silver crown. It was thicker than Tania's, obviously meant for Hugh. "We made this for our king."

Tania took the crown and placed it on his head. "My king. My husband."

Hugh touched her face. "My queen. My wife."

The faeries cheered.

Tania winked playfully, her wings flapping as she flew backwards, leading him. Hugh walked, his wings still hidden. It had been hard telling Thomas and William he'd not go back, but they understood he couldn't. He promised to keep in better touch than Juliana had. None of them knew what to do about their sister, but it was something that would never be far from their thoughts.

William had snickered when Hugh admitted to Tania's love turning him into a faery. Thomas had merely shook his head, looking sad even as he'd accepted what fate gave them.

When they were alone, she said, "I saw you ride into Bellemare. How is it you are here?"

"Prince Ladon," Hugh answered.

"The Tegwen prince?"

Hugh nodded.

"I do not understand. He is alive?"

"William saved him from Lucien's dungeon. He was here when William came for me."

"I did not see," Tania pulled him harder, making him quicken his pace up the stairs. "I was not myself."

Reading the pain in her eyes, he shook his head. "It's all in the past. We start anew. The two of us. I know you didn't mean any harm and I'm sorry for every harsh word I ever said to you and for every harsh action. I love you, my queen. This is where I want to be."

"But, I still do not understand how you are here. How is it Ladon took your place? I saw you walking into Bellemare, not he."

"Merrick used magic to make him like me. Shapechanging, he called it. Ladon has taken my place and will pose as the Earl of Bellemare until things are set right with the horses and so Thomas can be legally named my successor. It will assure that Bellemare stays in the family."

"And Ladon?" They reached the top of the stairwell and Tania didn't stop. She continued to face him, flying backward without glancing behind her as she navigated her way. "His family is here. Why does he go? Is it to repay William for saving him?"

Hugh reached for his shirt and she let go of him as he pulled it over his head. "Merrick feels Ladon will be safest in the mortal realm, where Lucien cannot go. Ladon sent word to King

Ean about it, but it was Ladon's choice to make. At Bellemare he will be surrounded by the blessed, but also the powerless. Ladon's powers are weakened, as is his body, and he needs time to heal both. Thomas will help him pretend to be me. Honestly, I find the whole idea strange—a man playing the role of me—but it is a good plan. When Ladon regains the memories he has lost and is ready to rejoin his people, his mortal death—or rather my death—will be faked or he'll leave on campaign where news of my death will be sent back to Bellemare. The details on that point are still hazy."

"You are amazing, Hugh. You have it all worked out."

"Aye, it is all arranged." Hugh nodded. He kept walking, past the bed toward the bathing pool. The clothes melted off her body. Tania gasped, looking down. "I did not—"

"I did." Hugh laughed, pulling her naked body close. "I have to admit. I am going to like having some of these powers."

"And the wings?" She looked over his shoulder to where they were still missing.

"Let us leave them be for now. Let me get used to one change at a time. First, I will learn of these new powers I have, learn to control them, learn to put you under my euphoric spell."

Tania giggled as they lowered into the pool. Warm water surrounded him, but it was nothing to the caress of his wife's body. As she leaned in to kiss him, all he saw was her. Everything would work out. He believed that now. Happiness and contentment was his, at least in this moment.

"I have been under your spell since the first moment I saw you, my king," Tania answered lovingly. "I will always be under your spell."

# About the Author

Michelle has always had an active imagination. Ever since she can remember, she's had a strange fascination with anything supernatural. She is married (madly in love) and has a wonderful family. To learn more about Michelle M Pillow's Samhain Publishing titles or the Realm Immortal series, please visit her website at www.michellepillow.com. Send an email to Michelle at michelle_pillow@yahoo.com or http://groups.yahoo.com/group/michellempillow/join.or join her Newsletter to learn of upcoming and current releases! www.michellepillow.com/newsletter/?p=subscribe

*The choice is simple: go with him or die.*

## King of the Unblessed

### © 2009 Michelle M. Pillow

*Realm Immortal, Book One*

Merrick, dark elfin King of Valdis, had once been heir to all that was good—happiness and pleasure his domain. Now, trapped as the ruler of mischief, king of necessary evil, he stands on a precipice of choice. On one side, his estranged brother, now ruler of what should have been Merrick's and, on the other, King Lucien of the Damned. Both would sway him. Damnation is winning.

Lady Juliana of Bellemare is from a human family, protected by the Blessed, coveted by the Damned. Betrothed to an old friend of her father's, Juliana is resigned to living out her days close to her childhood home, longing for an adventure, never dreaming she'd get what she wished for. When her fiancé is murdered and the children of Bellemare are stolen, Juliana is sent on a quest in a strange realm where appearances are deceiving.

Merrick brings more adventure and passion than any woman could want. Can she withstand the temptations of the Unblessed king? The spell she weaves over him is more than he can resist and, desperate to be the one to rule her, Merrick offers her a choice; either come with him until he tires of her…or die.

*Warning: This book contains hot sex, violence, trickster goblins, overly helpful sprights, a king of necessary evil who lives to get his way and a woman who would dare to deny him.*

*This title was previously released by Samhain Publishing.*

*To gain the only thing he truly wants,*
*he'll have to risk everything.*

## Stone Queen

*© 2009 Michelle M. Pillow*

*Realm Immortal, Book Three*

Juliana, newly appointed Queen of the Unblessed, has realized there is a bit more to her position than she first thought. Sure, it has its perks: a sinfully sexy husband who is also a king, growing powers and a magical life that's never boring, but the drawbacks are considerable. To save her kingdom from war, Juliana accepts assistance from a witch. But when her reality turns upside down, she realizes she's been betrayed.

For a brief time, Merrick knew happiness, as much happiness as the king of necessary evil could ever feel. Juliana has become the light in his darkness. Though he can never tell his wife he loves her—or risk upsetting the balance of both the mortal and immortal realms—the words are understood between them. Or so he thought. When she falls prey to a wayward spell, becoming encased in stone, he knows he'll have to risk everything to gain the only thing he truly wants.

*This book contains hot sex, violence, an evil witch, a blundering wizard, meddling sprights, a new queen and the lustful king who plans on showing her just how fun it is to be in charge.*

*This title was previously released by Samhain Publishing.*

My Bookstore & More
www.mybookstoreandmore.com
Green for the planet.
Great for your wallet.

LaVergne, TN USA
06 January 2011
211398LV00003B/79/P